Penguin Books

A Tree of Night and Oth[...]

D0525231

Truman Capote says of himself: 'I was born in New
Orleans in 1924 and raised in various parts of the South
– winters in New Orleans, summers in Alabama and
Georgia. I learned to read at a pre-school age. I
have always lived the life I liked. I have never skipped
a pulse beat over what others thought. My education
has been rather do-it-yourself. To this day I cannot
recite the alphabet or the multiplication tables. I had
already started writing short stories when I was 14
and some of them were published. I left school when I
was 15. My first – and last – regular job was with the
New Yorker when I was 17. Later, I "retired" to a
Louisiana farm for two years and wrote *Other Voices,
Other Rooms*. I have lived, at one time or another, in
Greece, Italy, Spain, Africa, and the West Indies and
travelled in Russia and the Orient.'

Other Voices, Other Rooms, Breakfast at Tiffany's and
The Grass Harp have been published in Penguins. *In Cold
Blood* was published in 1966 and immediately became the
centre of a storm of controversy. It has also been published
by Penguins and was filmed. His latest works are *The
Thanksgiving Visitor* (1969) and *The Dogs Bark* (1973).

Truman Capote

A Tree of Night and Other Stories

Penguin Books

Penguin Books Ltd, Harmondsworth,
Middlesex, England
Penguin Books, 625 Madison Avenue,
New York, New York 10022, U.S.A.
Penguin Books Australia Ltd, Ringwood,
Victoria, Australia
Penguin Books Canada Ltd, 2801 John Street,
Markham, Ontario, Canada L3R 1B4
Penguin Books (N.Z.) Ltd, 182–190 Wairau Road,
Auckland 10, New Zealand

First published in the U.S.A. 1949
Published in Great Britain by William Heinemann Ltd 1950
Six of these stories appear in *Selected Writings of Truman Capote*,
published by Hamish Hamilton 1963
Published in Penguin Books 1967
Reprinted 1971, 1978
Copyright 1949 by Truman Capote
All rights reserved

Made and printed in Great Britain by
C. Nicholls & Company Ltd
Set in Monotype Times

Contents

Master Misery 5

Children on Their Birthdays 26

Shut a Final Door 46

Jug of Silver 62

Miriam 77

The Headless Hawk 90

My Side of the Matter 115

A Tree of Night 126

Master Misery

Her high heels, clacking across the marble foyer, made her think of ice cubes rattling in a glass, and the flowers, those autumn chrysanthemums in the urn at the entrance, if touched they would shatter, splinter, she was sure, into frozen dust; yet the house was warm, even somewhat overheated, but cold, and Sylvia shivered, but cold, like the snowy swollen wastes of the secretary's face: Miss Mozart, who dressed all in white, as though she were a nurse. Perhaps she really was; that, of course, could be the answer. Mr Revercomb, you are mad, and this is your nurse; she thought about it for a moment: well, no. And now the butler brought her scarf. His beauty touched her: slender, so gentle, a Negro with freckled skin and reddish, unreflecting eyes. As he opened the door, Miss Mozart appeared, her starched uniform rustling dryly in the hall. 'We hope you will return,' she said, and handed Sylvia a sealed envelope. 'Mr Revercomb was most particularly pleased.'

Outside, dusk was falling like blue flakes, and Sylvia walked crosstown along the November streets until she reached the lonely upper reaches of Fifth Avenue. It occurred to her then that she might walk home through the park: an act of defiance almost, for Henry and Estelle, always insistent upon their city wisdom, had said over and again, Sylvia, you have no idea how dangerous it is, walking in the park after dark; look what happened to Myrtle Calisher. This isn't Easton, honey. That was the other thing they said. And said. God, she was sick of it. Still, and aside from a few of the other typists at SnugFare, an underwear company for which she worked, who else in New York did she know? Oh, it would be all right if only she did not have to live with them, if she could afford somewhere a small

5

room of her own; but there in that chintz-cramped apartment she sometimes felt she would choke them both. And why did she come to New York? For whatever reason, and it was indeed becoming vague, a principal cause of leaving Easton had been to rid herself of Henry and Estelle; or rather, their counterparts, though in point of fact Estelle was actually from Easton, a town north of Cincinnati. She and Sylvia had grown up together. The real trouble with Henry and Estelle was that they were so excruciatingly married. Nambypamby, bootsytotsy, and everything had a name: the telephone was Tinkling Tillie, the sofa, Our Nellie, the bed, Big Bear; yes, and what about those His-Her towels, those He-She pillows? Enough to drive you loony. 'Loony!' she said aloud, the quiet park erasing her voice. It was lovely now, and she was right to have walked here, with wind moving through the leaves, and globe lamps, freshly aglow, kindling the chalk drawings of children, pink birds, blue arrows, green hearts. But suddenly, like a pair of obscene words, there appeared on the path two boys: pimple-faced, grinning, they loomed in the dusk like menacing flames, and Sylvia, passing them, felt a burning all through her, quite as though she'd brushed fire. They turned and followed her past a deserted playground, one of them bump-bumping a stick along an iron fence, the other whistling: these sounds accumulated around her like the gathering roar of an oncoming engine, and when one of the boys, with a laugh, called, 'Hey, whatsa hurry?' her mouth twisted for breath. Don't, she thought, thinking to throw down her purse and run. At that moment, a man walking a dog came up a sidepath, and she followed at his heels to the exit. Wouldn't they feel gratified, Henry and Estelle, wouldn't they we-told-you-so if she were to tell them? and, what is more, Estelle would write it home and the next thing you knew it would be all over Easton that she'd been raped in Central Park. She spent the rest of the way home despising New York: anonymity, its virtuous terror; and the squeaking drainpipe, all-night light, ceaseless footfall, subway corridor, numbered door (3C).

'Shh, honey,' Estelle said, sidling out of the kitchen, 'Bootsy's doing his homework.' Sure enough, Henry, a law student at Columbia, was hunched over his books in the living-room, and Sylvia, at Estelle's request, took off her shoes before tiptoeing through. Once inside her room, she threw herself on the bed and put her hands over her eyes. Had today really happened? Miss Mozart and Mr Revercomb, were they really there in the tall house on Seventy-eighth Street?

'So, honey, what happened today?' Estelle had entered without knocking.

Sylvia sat up on her elbow. 'Nothing. Except that I typed ninety-seven letters.'

'About what, honey?' asked Estelle, using Sylvia's hairbrush.

'Oh, hell, what do you suppose? SnugFare, the shorts that safely support our leaders of Science and Industry.'

'Gee, honey, don't sound so cross. I don't know what's wrong with you sometimes. You sound so cross. Ouch! Why don't you get a new brush? This one's just knotted with hair....'

'Mostly yours.'

'What did you say?'

'Skip it.'

'Oh, I thought you said something. Anyway, like I was saying, I wish you didn't have to go to that office and come home every day feeling cross and out of sorts. Personally, and I said this to Bootsy just last night and he agreed with me one hundred per cent, I said, Bootsy, I think Sylvia ought to get married: a girl high-strung like that needs her tensions relaxed. There's no earthly reason why you shouldn't. I mean maybe you're not pretty in the ordinary sense, but you have beautiful eyes, and an intelligent, really sincere look. In fact you're the sort of girl any professional man would be lucky to get. And I should think you would want to.... Look what a different person I am since I married Henry. Doesn't it make you lonesome seeing how happy we are? I'm here to tell you, honey, that there is nothing like lying in bed at night with a man's arms around you and ...'

'Estelle! For Christ's sake!' Sylvia sat bolt upright in bed, anger on her cheeks like rouge. But after a moment she bit her lip and lowered her eyelids. 'I'm sorry,' she said, 'I didn't mean to shout. Only I wish you wouldn't talk like that.'

'It's all right,' said Estelle, smiling in a dumb, puzzled way. Then she went over and gave Sylvia a kiss. 'I understand, honey. It's just that you're plain worn out. And I'll bet you haven't had anything to eat either. Come on in the kitchen and I'll scramble you some eggs.'

When Estelle set the eggs before her, Sylvia felt quite ashamed; after all, Estelle was trying to be nice; and so then, as though to make it all up, she said: 'Something did happen today.'

Estelle sat down across from her with a cup of coffee, and Sylvia went on: 'I don't know how to tell about it. It's so odd. But – well, I had lunch at the Automat today, and I had to share the table with these three men. I might as well have been invisible because they talked about the most personal things. One of the men said his girl friend was going to have a baby and he didn't know where he was going to get the money to do anything about it. So one of the other men asked him why didn't he sell something. He said he didn't have anything to sell. Whereupon the third man (he was rather delicate and didn't look as if he belonged with the others) said yes, there was something he could sell: *dreams*. Even I laughed, but the man shook his head and said very seriously: no, it was perfectly true, his wife's aunt, Miss Mozart, worked for a rich man who bought dreams, regular night-time dreams – from anybody. And he wrote down the man's name and address and gave it to his friend; but the man simply left it lying on the table. It was too crazy for him, he said.'

'Me, too,' Estelle put in a little righteously.

'I don't know,' said Sylvia, lighting a cigarette. 'But I couldn't get it out of my head. The name written on the paper was A. F. Revercomb and the address was on East Seventy-eighth Street. I only glanced at it for a moment, but it was . . . I don't know, I couldn't seem to forget it. It was beginning to give me a headache. So I left the office early . . .'

Slowly and with emphasis, Estelle put down her coffee cup.

'Honey, listen, you don't mean you went to see him, this Revercomb nut?'

'I didn't mean to,' she said, immediately embarrassed. To try and tell about it she now realized was a mistake. Estelle had no imagination, she would never understand. So her eyes narrowed, the way they always did when she composed a lie. 'And, as a matter of fact, I didn't,' she said flatly. 'I started to; but then I realized how silly it was, and went for a walk instead.'

'That was sensible of you,' said Estelle as she began stacking dishes in the kitchen sink. 'Imagine what might have happened. Buying dreams! Whoever heard! Uh uh, honey, this sure isn't Easton.'

Before retiring, Sylvia took a seconal, something she seldom did; but she knew otherwise she would never rest, not with her mind so nimble and somersaulting; then, too, she felt a curious sadness, a sense of loss, as though she'd been the victim of some real or even moral theft, as though, in fact, the boys encountered in the park had snatched (abruptly she switched on the light) her purse. The envelope Miss Mozart had handed her: it was in the purse, and until now she had forgotten it. She tore it open. Inside there was a blue note folded around a bill; on the note there was written: *In payment of one dream*, $5. And now she believed it; it was true, and she had sold Mr Revercomb a dream. Could it be really so simple as that? She laughed a little as she turned off the light again. If she were to sell a dream only twice a week, think of what she could do: a place somewhere all her own, she thought, deepening towards sleep; ease, like firelight, wavered over her, and there came the moment of twilit lantern slides, deeply deeper. His lips, his arms: telescoped, descending; and distastefully she kicked away the blanket. Were these cold man-arms the arms Estelle had spoken of? Mr Revercomb's lips brushed her ear as he leaned far into her sleep. Tell me? he whispered.

It was a week before she saw him again, a Sunday afternoon in early December. She'd left the apartment intending to see a movie, but somehow, and as though it had happened without her knowledge, she found herself on Madison Avenue, two blocks from Mr Revercomb's. It was a cold, silver-skied day, with winds sharp and catching as hollyhock; in store windows icicles of Christmas tinsel twinkled amid mounds of sequined snow: all to Sylvia's distress, for she hated holidays, those times when one is most alone. In one window she saw a spectacle which made her stop still. It was a life-sized, mechanical Santa Claus; slapping his stomach he rocked back and forth in a frenzy of electrical mirth. You could hear beyond the thick glass his squeaky uproarious laughter. The longer she watched the more evil he seemed, until, finally, with a shudder, she turned and made her way into the street of Mr Revercomb's house. It was, from the outside, an ordinary town house, perhaps a trifle less polished, less imposing than some others, but relatively grand all the same. Winter-withered ivy writhed about the leaded windowpanes and trailed in octopus ropes over the door; at the sides of the door were two small stone lions with blind, chipped eyes. Sylvia took a breath, then rang the bell. Mr Revercomb's pale and charming Negro recognized her with a courteous smile.

On the previous visit, the parlour in which she had awaited her audience with Mr Revercomb had been empty except for herself. This time there were others present, women of several appearances, and an excessively nervous, gnat-eyed young man. Had this group been what it resembled, namely, patients in a doctor's anteroom, he would have seemed either an expectant father or a victim of St Vitus. Sylvia was seated next to him, and his fidgety eyes unbuttoned her rapidly: whatever he saw apparently intrigued him very little, and Sylvia was grateful when he went back to his twitchy preoccupations. Gradually, though, she became conscious of how interested in her the assemblage seemed; in the dim, doubtful light of the plant-filled room their gazes were more rigid than the chairs upon which they sat; one woman was particularly relentless. Ordinarily, her face would have had a soft commonplace sweetness, but now, watching Sylvia, it was ugly with distrust, jealousy. As though trying to tame some creature which might suddenly spring full-fanged, she sat stroking a flea-bitten neck fur, her stare continuing its assault until the earthquake footstep of

Miss Mozart was heard in the hall. Immediately, and like frightened students, the group, separating into their individual identities, came to attention. 'You, Mr Pocker,' accused Miss Mozart, 'you're next!' and Mr Pocker, wringing his hands, jittering his eyes, followed after her. In the dusk-room the gathering settled again like sun motes.

It began then to rain; melting window reflections quivered on the walls, and Mr Revercomb's young butler, seeping through the room, stirred a fire in the grate, set tea things upon a table. Sylvia, nearest the fire, felt drowsy with warmth and the noise of rain; her head tilted sideways, she closed her eyes, neither asleep nor really awake. For a long while only the crystal swingings of a clock scratched the polished silence of Mr Revercomb's house. And then, abruptly, there was an enormous commotion in the hall, capsizing the room into a fury of sound: a bull-deep voice, vulgar as red, roared out: 'Stop Oreilly? The ballet butler and who else?' The owner of this voice, a tub-shaped, brick-coloured little man, shoved his way to the parlour threshold, where he stood drunkenly see-sawing from foot to foot. 'Well, well, well,' he said, his gin-hoarse voice descending the scale, 'and all these ladies before me? But Oreilly is a gentleman, Oreilly waits his turn.'

'Not here, he doesn't,' said Miss Mozart, stealing up behind him and seizing him sternly by the collar. His face went even redder and his eyes bubbled out: 'You're choking me,' he gasped, but Miss Mozart, whose green-pale hands were as strong as oak roots, jerked his tie still tighter, and propelled him towards the door, which presently slammed with shattering effect: a tea cup tinkled, and dry dahlia leaves tumbled from their heights. The lady with the fur slipped an aspirin into her mouth. 'Dis*gusting*,' she said, and the others, all except Sylvia, laughed delicately, admiringly, as Miss Mozart strode past dusting her hands.

It was raining thick and darkly when Sylvia left Mr Revercomb's. She looked around the desolate street for a taxi; there was nothing, however, and no one; yes, someone, the drunk man who had caused the disturbance. Like a lonely city child, he was leaning against a parked car and bouncing a rubber ball up and down 'Lookit, kid,' he said to Sylvia, 'lookit, I just found this ball. Do you suppose that means good luck?' Sylvia smiled at him; for all his bravado, she thought him rather harmless, and there was a quality in his face, some grinning sadness suggesting a clown minus make-up. Juggling his ball, he skipped along after her as she headed toward Madison Avenue. 'I'll bet I made a fool of myself in there,' he said. 'When I do things like that I just want to sit down and cry.' Standing so long in the rain seemed to have sobered him considerably. 'But she ought not to have choked me that way; damn, she's too rough. I've known some rough women: my sister Berenice could brand the wildest bull; but that other one, she's the roughest of the lot. Mark Oreilly's word, she's going to end up in the electric chair,' he said, and smacked his lips. 'They've got no cause to treat me like that. It's every bit his fault anyhow. I didn't have an awful lot to begin with, but then he took it every bit, and now I've got *niente*, kid, *niente*.'

'That's too bad,' said Sylvia, though she did not know what she was being sympathetic about. 'Are you a clown, Mr Oreilly?'

'Was,' he said.

By this time they had reached the avenue, but Sylvia did not even look for a taxi; she wanted to walk on in the rain with the man who had been a clown. 'When I was a little girl I only liked clown dolls,' she told him. 'My room at home was like a circus.'

'I've been other things besides a clown. I have sold insurance, too.'

'Oh?' said Sylvia, disappointed. 'And what do you do now?'

Oreilly chuckled and threw his ball especially high; after the catch his head still remained tilted upward. 'I watch the sky,' he said. 'There I am with my suitcase travelling through the blue. It's where you travel when you've got no place else to go. But what do I do on this planet? I have stolen, begged, and sold my dreams – all for purposes of whiskey. A man cannot travel in the blue without a bottle. Which brings us to a point: how'd you take it, baby, if I asked for the loan of a dollar?'

'I'd take it fine,' Sylvia replied, and paused, uncertain of what she'd say next. They wandered along so slowly, the stiff rain enclosing them like an insulating pressure; it was as though she were walking with a childhood doll, one grown miraculous and capable; she reached and held his hand: dear clown travelling in the blue. 'But I haven't got a dollar. All I've got is seventy cents.'

'No hard feelings,' said Oreilly. 'But honest, is that the kind of money he's paying nowadays?'

Sylvia knew whom he meant. 'No, no – as a matter of fact, I didn't sell him a dream.' She made no attempt to explain; she didn't understand it herself. Confronting the greying invisibility of Mr Revercomb (impeccable, exact as a scale, surrounded in a cologne of clinical odours; flat grey eyes planted like seed in the anonymity of his face and sealed within steel-dull lenses) she could not remember a dream, and so she told of two thieves who had chased her through the park and in and out among the swings of a playground. 'Stop, he said for me to stop; there are dreams and dreams, he said, but that is not a real one, that is one you are making up. Now how do you suppose he knew that? So I told him another dream; it was about him, of how he held me in the night with balloons rising and moons falling all around. He said he was not interested in dreams concerning himself.' Miss Mozart, who transcribed the dreams in shorthand, was told to call the next person. 'I don't think I will go back there again,' she said.

'You will,' said Oreilly. 'Look at me, even I go back, and he has long since finished with me, Master Misery.'

'Master Misery? Why do you call him that?'

They had reached the corner where the maniacal Santa Claus rocked and bellowed. His laughter echoed in the rainy squeaking street, and a shadow of him swayed in the rainbow lights of the pavement. Oreilly, turning his back upon the Santa Claus, smiled and said: 'I call him Master Misery on account of that's who he is. Master Misery. Only maybe you call him something else; anyway, he is the same fellow, and you must've known him. All mothers tell their kids about him: he lives in hollows of trees, he comes down chimneys late at night, he lurks in graveyards and you can hear his step in the attic. The sonofabitch, he is a thief and a threat: he will take everything you have and end by leaving you nothing, not even a dream. Boo!' he shouted, and laughed louder than Santa Claus. 'Now do you know who he is?'

Sylvia nodded. 'I know who he is. My family called him something else. But I can't remember what. It was long ago.'

'But you remember him?'

'Yes, I remember him.'

'Then call him Master Misery,' he said, and, bouncing his ball, walked away from her. 'Master Misery,' his voice trailed to a mere moth of sound, 'Mas-ter Mis-er-y . . .'

It was hard to look at Estelle, for she was in front of a window, and the window was filled with windy sun, which hurt Sylvia's eyes, and the glass rattled, which hurt her head. Also, Estelle was lecturing. Her nasal voice sounded as though her throat were a depository of rusty razor blades. 'I wish you could see yourself,' she was saying. Or was that something she'd said a long while back? Never mind. 'I don't know what's happened to you: I'll bet you don't weigh a hundred pounds, I can see every bone and vein, and your hair! You look like a poodle.'

Sylvia passed a hand over her forehead. 'What time is it, Estelle?'

'It's four,' she said, interrupting herself long enough to look at her watch. 'But where is your watch?'

'I sold it,' said Sylvia, too tired to lie. It did not matter. She had sold so many things, including her beaver coat and gold mesh evening bag.

Estelle shook her head. 'I give up, honey, I plain give up. And that was the watch your mother gave you for graduation. It's a shame,' she said, and made an old-maid noise with her mouth, 'a pity and a shame. I'll never understand why you left us. That is your business, I'm sure; only how could you have left us for this . . . this . . . ?'

'Dump,' supplied Sylvia, using the word advisedly. It was a furnished room in the East Sixties between Second and Third Avenues. Large enough for a daybed and a splintery old

14

bureau with a mirror like a cataracted eye, it had one window, which looked out on a vast vacant lot (you could hear the tough afternoon voices of desperate running boys) and in the distance, like an exclamation point for the skyline, there was the black smokestack of a factory. This smokestack occurred frequently in her dreams; it never failed to arouse Miss Mozart: 'Phallic, phallic,' she would mutter, glancing up from her shorthand. The floor of the room was a garbage pail of books begun but never finished, antique newspapers, even orange hulls, fruit cores, underwear, a spilled powder box.

Estelle kicked her way through this trash, and sat down on the daybed. 'Honey, you don't know, but I've been worried crazy. I mean I've got pride and all that and if you don't like me, well o.k.; but you've got no right to stay away like this and not let me hear from you in over a month. So today I said to Bootsy, Bootsy I've got a feeling something terrible has happened to Sylvia. You can imagine how I felt when I called your office and they told me you hadn't worked there for the last four weeks. What happened, were you fired?'

'Yes, I was fired.' Sylvia began to sit up. 'Please, Estelle – I've got to get ready; I've got an appointment.'

'Be still. You're not going anywhere till I know what's wrong. The landlady downstairs told me you were found sleep-walking. . . .'

'What do you mean talking to her? Why are you spying on me?'

Estelle's eyes puckered, as though she were going to cry. She put her hand over Sylvia's and petted it gently. 'Tell me, honey, is it because of a man?'

'It's because of a man, yes,' said Sylvia, laughter at the edge of her voice.

'You should have come to me before,' Estelle sighed. 'I know about men. That is nothing for you to be ashamed of. A man can have a way with a woman that kind of makes her forget everything else. If Henry wasn't the fine upstanding potential lawyer that he is, why, I would still love him, and do things for him that before I knew what it was like to be with a man would have seemed shocking and horrible. But honey,

15

this fellow you've mixed up with, he's taking advantage of you.'

'It's not that kind of relationship,' said Sylvia, getting up and locating a pair of stockings in the *furor* of her bureau drawers. 'It hasn't got anything to do with love. Forget about it. In fact, go home and forget about me altogether.'

Estelle looked at her narrowly. 'You scare me, Sylvia; you really scare me.' Sylvia laughed and went on getting dressed. 'Do you remember a long time ago when I said you ought to get married?'

'Uh huh. And now you listen.' Sylvia turned around; there was a row of hairpins spaced across her mouth; she extracted them one at a time all the while she talked. 'You talk about getting married as though it were the answer absolute; very well, up to a point I agree. Sure, I want to be loved; who the hell doesn't? But even if I was willing to compromise, where is the man I'm going to marry? Believe me, he must've fallen down a manhole. I mean it seriously when I say there are no men in New York – and even if there were, how do you meet them? Every man I ever met here who seemed the slightest bit attractive was either married, too poor to get married, or queer. And anyway, this is no place to fall in love; this is where you ought to come when you want to get over being in love. Sure, I suppose I could marry somebody; but I do not want that. Do I?'

Estelle shrugged. 'Then what do you want?'

'More than is coming to me.' She poked the last hairpin into place, and smoothed her eyebrows before the mirror. 'I have an appointment, Estelle, and it is time for you to go now.'

'I can't leave you like this,' said Estelle, her hand waving helplessly around the room. 'Sylvia, you were my childhood friend.'

'That is just the point: we're not children any more; at least, I'm not. No, I want you to go home, and I don't want you to come here again. I just want you to forget about me.'

Estelle fluttered at her eyes with a handkerchief, and by the time she reached the door she was weeping quite loudly. Sylvia could not afford remorse: having been mean, there was nothing to be but meaner. 'Go on,' she said, following Estelle into the hall, 'and write home any damn nonsense about me you want to!' Letting out a wail that brought other roomers to their doors, Estelle fled down the stairs.

After this Sylvia went back into her room and sucked a piece of sugar to take the sour taste out of her mouth: it was her grandmother's remedy for bad tempers. Then she got down on her knees and pulled from under the bed a cigar box she kept hidden there. When you opened the box it played a home-made and somewhat disorganized version of 'Oh How I Hate to Get up in the Morning.' Her brother had made the music-box and given it to her on her fourteenth birthday. Eating the sugar, she'd thought of her grandmother, and hearing the tune she thought of her brother; the rooms of the house where they had lived rotated before her, all dark and she like a light moving among them: up the stairs, down, out and through, spring sweet and lilac shadows in the air and the creaking of a porch swing. All gone, she thought, calling their names, and now I am absolutely alone. The music stopped. But it went on in her head; she could hear it bugling above the child-cries of the vacant lot. And it interfered with her reading. She was reading a little diary-like book she kept inside the box. In this book she wrote down the essentials of her dreams; they were endless now, and it was so hard to remember. Today she would tell Mr Revercomb about the three blind children. He would like that. The prices he paid varied, and she was sure this was at least a ten-dollar dream. The cigar-box anthem followed her down the stairs and through the streets and she longed for it to go away.

In the store where Santa Claus had been there was a new and equally unnerving exhibit. Even when she was late to Mr Revercomb's, as now, Sylvia was compelled to pause by the window. A plaster girl with intense glass eyes sat astride a bicycle pedalling at the maddest pace; though its wheel spokes spun hypnotically, the bicycle of course never budged: all that effort and the poor girl going nowhere. It was a pitifully human situation, and one that Sylvia could so exactly identify with herself that she always felt a real pang. The music-box rewound in her head: the tune, her brother, the house, a high-school dance, the house, the tune! Couldn't Mr Revercomb hear it? His penetrating gaze carried such dull suspicion. But he seemed pleased with her dream, and, when she left, Miss Mozart gave her an envelope containing ten dollars.

'I had a ten-dollar dream,' she told Oreilly, and Oreilly, rubbing his hands together, said, 'Fine! Fine! But that's just my luck, baby – you should've got here sooner 'cause I went and did a terrible thing. I walked into a liquor store up the street, snatched a quart and ran.' Sylvia didn't believe him until he produced from his pinned-together overcoat a bottle of bourbon, already half gone. 'You're going to get in trouble some day,' she said, 'and then what would happen to me? I don't know what I would do without you.' Oreilly laughed and poured a shot of the whiskey into a water glass. They were sitting in an all-night cafeteria, a great glaring food depot alive with blue mirrors and raw murals. Although to Sylvia it seemed a sordid place, they met there frequently for dinner; but even if she could have afforded it she did not know where else they could go, for together they presented a curious aspect: a young girl and a doddering, drunken man. Even here people often stared at them; if they stared long enough, Oreilly would stiffen with dignity and say: 'Hello, hot lips, I remember you from way back. Still working in the men's room?' But usually they were left to themselves, and sometimes they would sit talking until two and three in the morning.

'It's a good thing the rest of Master Misery's crowd don't know he gave you that ten bucks. One of them would say you stole the dream. I had that happen once. Eaten up, all of 'em, never saw such a bunch of sharks, worse than actors or clowns or businessmen. Crazy, if you think about it: you worry whether you're going to go to sleep, if you're going to have a dream, if you're going to remember the dream. Round and round. So you get a couple of bucks, so you rush to the nearest liquor store – or the nearest sleeping-pill machine. And first thing you know, you're roaming your way up outhouse alley. Why, baby, you know what it's like? It's just like life.'

'No, Oreilly, that's what it isn't like. It hasn't anything to do with life. It has more to do with being dead. I feel as though everything were being taken from me, as though some thief were stealing me down to the bone. Oreilly, I tell you I haven't an ambition, and there used to be so much. I don't understand it and I don't know what to do.'

He grinned. 'And you say it isn't like life? Who understands life and who knows what to do?'

'Be serious,' she said. 'Be serious and put away that whiskey and eat your soup before it gets stone cold.' She lighted a cigarette, and the smoke, smarting her eyes, intensified her frown. 'If only I knew what he wanted with those dreams, all typed and filed. What does he do with them? You're right when you say he is Master Misery. . . . He can't be simply some silly quack; it can't be so meaningless as that. But why does he want dreams? Help me, Oreilly, think, think: what does it mean?'

Squinting one eye, Oreilly poured himself another drink; the clownlike twist of his mouth hardened into a line of scholarly straightness. 'That is a million-dollar question, kid. Why don't you ask something easy, like how to cure the common cold? Yes, kid, what does it mean? I have thought about it a good deal. I have thought about it in the process of making love to a woman, and I have thought about it in the middle of a poker game.' He tossed the drink down his throat and shuddered. 'Now a sound can start a dream; the noise of one car passing in the night can drop a hundred sleepers into the deep parts of themselves. It's funny to think of that one car racing through the dark, trailing so many dreams. Sex, a sudden change of light, a pickle, these are little keys that can open up our insides, too. But most dreams begin because there are furies inside of us that blow open all the doors. I don't believe in Jesus Christ, but I do believe in people's souls; and I figure it this way, baby: dreams are the mind of the soul and the secret truth about us. Now Master Misery, maybe he hasn't got a soul, so bit by bit he borrows yours, steals it like he would steal your dolls or the chicken wing off your plate. Hundreds of souls have passed through him and gone into a filing case.'

'Oreilly, be serious,' she said again, annoyed because she thought he was making more jokes. 'And look, your soup is . . .' She stopped abruptly, startled by Oreilly's peculiar expression. He was looking toward the entrance. Three men were there, two policemen and a civilian wearing a clerk's cloth jacket. The clerk was pointing toward their table. Oreilly's eyes circled the room with trapped despair; he sighed then, and leaned back in his seat, ostentatiously pouring himself another drink. 'Good evening, gentlemen,' he said, when the official party confronted him, 'will you join us for a drink?'

'You can't arrest him,' cried Sylvia, 'you can't arrest a clown!' She threw her ten-dollar bill at them, but the policemen did not pay any attention, and she began to pound the table. All the customers in the place were staring, and the manager came running up, wringing his hands. The police said for Oreilly to get to his feet. 'Certainly,' Oreilly said, 'though I do think it shocking you have to trouble yourselves with such petty crimes as mine when everywhere there are master thieves afoot. For instance, this pretty child,' he stepped between the officers and pointed to Sylvia, 'she is the recent victim of a major theft: poor baby, she has had her soul stolen.'

For two days following Oreilly's arrest Sylvia did not leave her room: sun on the window, then dark. By the third day she had run out of cigarettes, so she ventured as far as the corner delicatessen. She bought a package of cupcakes, a can of sardines, a newspaper and cigarettes. In all this time she'd not eaten and it was a light, delicious, sharpening sensation; but the climb back up the stairs, the relief of closing the door, these so exhausted her she could not quite make the daybed. She slid down to the floor and did not move until it was day again. She thought afterwards that she'd been there about twenty minutes. Turning on the radio as loud as it would go, she dragged a chair up to the window and opened the newspaper on her lap: *Lana Denies, Russia Rejects, Miners Conciliate*: of all things this was saddest, that life goes on: if one leaves one's lover, life should stop for him, and if one disappears from the world, then the world should stop, too; and it never did. And that was the real reason for most people getting up in the morning: not because it would matter but because it wouldn't. But if Mr Revercomb succeeded finally in collecting all the dreams out of every head, perhaps – the idea slipped, became entangled with radio and newspaper. *Falling Temperatures*. A snowstorm moving across Colorado, across the West, falling upon all the small towns, yellowing every light, filling every footfall, falling now and here; but how quickly it had come, the snowstorm: the roofs, the vacant lot, the distance deep in white and deepening, like sheep. She looked at the paper and she looked at the snow. But it must have been snowing all day. It could not have just started. There was no sound of traffic; in the swirling wastes of the vacant lot children circled a bonfire; a car, buried at the kerb, winked its headlights: help, help! silent, like the heart's distress. She crumbled a cupcake and sprinkled it on the windowsill: north-birds would come to keep her company. And she left the window open for them; snow-wind scattered flakes that dissolved on the floor like April-fool jewels. *Presents Life Can Be Beautiful*: turn down that radio! The witch of the woods was tapping at her door: Yes, Mrs Halloran, she said, and turned off the radio altogether. Snow-quiet, sleep-silent, only the fun-fire faraway songsinging of children; and the room was blue with cold, colder than the cold of fairytales: lie down my heart among the igloo flowers of snow. Mr Revercomb, why do you wait upon the threshold? Ah, do come inside, it is so cold out there.

But her moment of waking was warm and held. The window was closed, and a man's arms were around her. He was singing to her, his voice gentle but jaunty: *cherryberry, moneyberry, happyberry pie, but the best old pie is a loveberry pie* . . .

'Oreilly, is it – is it really you?'

He squeezed her. 'Baby's awake now. And how does she feel?'

'I had thought I was dead,' she said, and happiness winged around inside her like a bird lamed but still flying. She tried to hug him and she was too weak. 'I love you, Oreilly; you are my only friend and I was so frightened. I thought I would never see you again.' She paused, remembering. 'But why aren't you in jail?'

Oreilly's face got all tickled and pink. 'I was never in jail,' he said mysteriously. 'But first, let's have something to eat. I brought some things up from the delicatessen this morning.'

She had a sudden feeling of floating. 'How long have you been here?'

'Since yesterday,' he said, fussing around with bundles and paper plates. 'You let me in yourself.'

'That's impossible. I don't remember it at all.'

'I know,' he said, leaving it at that. 'Here, drink your milk like a good kid and I'll tell you a real wicked story. Oh, it's wild,' he promised, slapping his sides gladly and looking more than ever like a clown. 'Well, like I said, I never was in jail and this bit of fortune came to me because there I was being hustled down the street by those bindlestiffs when who should I see come swinging along but the gorilla woman: you guessed it, Miss Mozart. Hi, I says to her, off to the barber shop for a shave? It's about time you were put under arrest, she says, and smiles at one of the cops. Do your duty, officer. Oh, I says to her, I'm not under arrest. Me, I'm just on my way to the station house to give them the lowdown on you, you dirty communist. You can imagine what sort of holler she set up then; she grabbed hold of me and the cops grabbed hold of her. Can't say I didn't warn them: careful, boys, I said, she's got hair on her chest. And she sure did lay about her. So I just sort of walked off down the street. Never have believed in standing around watching fist-fights the way people do in this city.'

Oreilly stayed with her in the room over the weekend. It was like the most beautiful party Sylvia could remember; she'd never laughed so much, for one thing, and no one, certainly no one in her family, had ever made her feel so loved. Oreilly was a fine cook, and he fixed delicious dishes on the little electric stove; once he scooped snow off the windowsill and made sherbet flavoured with strawberry syrup. By Sunday she was strong enough to dance. They turned on the radio and she danced until she fell to her knees, windless and laughing. 'I'll never be afraid again,' she said. 'I hardly know what I was afraid of to begin with.'

'The same things you'll be afraid of the next time,' Oreilly told her quietly. 'That is a quality of Master Misery: no one ever knows what he is – not even children, and they know mostly everything.'

Sylvia went to the window; an arctic whiteness lay over the city, but the snow had stopped, and the night sky was as clear as ice: there, riding above the river, she saw the first star of evening. 'I see the first star,' she said, crossing her fingers.

'And what do you wish when you see the first star?'

'I wish to see another star,' she said. 'At least that is what I usually wish.'

'But tonight?'

She sat down on the floor and leaned her head against his knee. 'Tonight I wished that I could have back my dreams.'

'Don't we all?' Oreilly said, stroking her hair. 'But then what would you do? I mean what would you do if you could have them back?'

Sylvia was silent a moment; when she spoke her eyes were gravely distant. 'I would go home,' she said slowly. 'And that is a terrible decision, for it would mean giving up most of my other dreams. But if Mr Revercomb would let me have them back, then I would go home tomorrow.'

Saying nothing, Oreilly went to the closet and brought back her coat. 'But why?' she asked as he helped her on with it. 'Never mind,' he said, 'just do what I tell you. We're going to pay Mr Revercomb a call, and you're going to ask him to give you back your dreams. It's a chance.'

Sylvia balked at the door. 'Please, Oreilly, don't make me go. I can't, please, I'm afraid.'

'I thought you said you'd never be afraid again.'

But once in the street he hurried her so quickly against the wind she did not have time to be frightened. It was Sunday, stores were closed and the traffic lights seemed to wink only for them, for there were no moving cars along the snow-deep avenue. Sylvia even forgot where they were going, and chattered of trivial oddments: right here at this corner is where she'd seen Garbo, and over there, that is where the old woman was run over. Presently, however, she stopped, out of breath and overwhelmed with sudden realization. 'I can't, Oreilly,' she said, pulling back. 'What can I say to him?'

'Make it like a business deal,' said Oreilly. 'Tell him straight out that you want your dreams, and if he'll give them to you you'll pay back all the money: on the instalment plan, naturally. It's simple enough, kid. Why the hell couldn't he give them back? They are all right there in a filing case.'

This speech was somehow convincing and, stamping her frozen feet, Sylvia went ahead with a certain courage. 'That's the kid,' he said. They separated on Third Avenue, Oreilly being of the opinion that Mr Revercomb's immediate neighbourhood was not for the moment precisely safe. He confined himself in a doorway, now and then lighting a match and singing aloud: *but the best old pie is a whiskeyberry pie!* Like a wolf, a long thin dog came padding over the moon-slats under the elevated, and across the street there were the misty shapes of men ganged around a bar: the idea of maybe cadging a drink in there made him groggy.

Just as he had decided on perhaps trying something of the sort, Sylvia appeared. And she was in his arms before he knew that it was really her. 'It can't be so bad, sweetheart,' he said softly, holding her as best he could. 'Don't cry, baby; it's too cold to cry: you'll chap your face.' As she strangled for words, her crying evolved into a tremulous, unnatural laugh. The air was filled with the smoke of her laughter. 'Do you know what he said?' she gasped. 'Do you know what he said when I asked for my dreams?' Her head fell back, and her laughter rose and carried over the street like an abandoned, wildly coloured kite. Oreilly had finally to shake her by the shoulders. 'He said – I couldn't have them back because – because he'd used them all up.'

She was silent then, her face smoothing into an expressionless calm. She put her arm through Oreilly's, and together they moved down the street; but it was as if they were friends pacing a platform, each waiting for the other's train, and when they reached the corner he cleared his throat and said: 'I guess I'd better turn off here. It's as likely a spot as any.'

Sylvia held on to his sleeve. 'But where will you go, Oreilly?'

'Travelling in the blue,' he said, trying a smile that didn't work out very well.

She opened her purse. 'A man cannot travel in the blue without a bottle,' she said, and kissing him on the cheek, slipped five dollars in his pocket.

'Bless you, baby.'

It did not matter that it was the last of her money, that now she would have to walk home, and alone. The pilings of snow were like the white waves of a white sea, and she rode upon them, carried by winds and tides of the moon. I do not know what I want, and perhaps I shall never know, but my only wish from every star will always be another star; and truly I am not afraid, she thought. Two boys came out of a bar and stared at her; in some park some long time ago she'd seen two boys and they might be the same. Truly I am not afraid, she thought, hearing their snowy footsteps following her; and anyway, there was nothing left to steal.

Children on Their Birthdays

(This Story is for Andrew Lyndon)

Yesterday afternoon the six-o'clock bus ran over Miss Bobbit. I'm not sure what there is to be said about it; after all, she was only ten years old, still I know no one of us in this town will forget her. For one thing, nothing she ever did was ordinary, not from the first time that we saw her, and that was a year ago. Miss Bobbit and her mother, they arrived on that same six-o'clock bus, the one that comes through from Mobile. It happened to be my cousin Billy Bob's birthday, and so most of the children in town were here at our house. We were sprawled off the front porch having tutti-frutti and devil cake when the bus stormed around Deadman's Curve. It was the summer that never rained; rusted dryness coated everything; sometimes when a car passed on the road, raised dust would hang in the still air an hour or more. Aunt El said if they didn't pave the highway soon she was going to move down to the seacoast; but she'd said that for such a long time. Anyway, we were sitting on the porch, tutti-frutti melting on our plates, when suddenly, just as we were wishing that something would happen, something did; for out of the red road dust appeared Miss Bobbit. A wiry little girl in a starched, lemon-coloured party dress, she sassed along with a grownup mince, one hand on her hip, the other supporting a spinsterish umbrella. Her mother, lugging two cardboard valises and a wind-up victrola, trailed in the background. She was a gaunt shaggy woman with silent eyes and a hungry smile.

All the children on the porch had grown so still that when a cone of wasps started humming the girls did not set up their usual holler. Their attention was too fixed upon the approach of Miss Bobbit and her mother, who had by now reached the gate. 'Begging your pardon,' called Miss Bobbit in a voice that was at once silky and childlike, like a pretty piece of ribbon, and immaculately exact, like a movie-star or a schoolmarm, 'but might we speak with the grownup persons of the house?' This, of course, meant Aunt El; and, at least to some degree, myself. But Billy Bob and all the other boys, no one of whom was over fourteen, followed down to the gate after us. From their faces you would have thought they'd never seen a girl before. Certainly not like Miss Bobbit. As Aunt El said, who-ever heard tell of a child wearing make-up? Tangee gave her lips an orange glow, her hair, rather like a costume wig, was a mass of rosy curls, and her eyes had a knowing pencilled tilt; even so, she had a skinny dignity, she was a lady, and, what is more, she looked you in the eye with manlike directness. 'I'm Miss Lily Jane Bobbit, Miss Bobbit from Memphis, Tennes-see,' she said solemnly. The boys looked down at their toes, and, on the porch, Cora McCall, who Billy Bob was courting at the time, led the girls into a fanfare of giggles. 'Country children,' said Miss Bobbit with an understanding smile, and gave her parasol a saucy whirl. 'My mother,' and this homely woman allowed an abrupt nod to acknowledge herself, 'my mother and I have taken rooms here. Would you be so kind as to point out the house? It belongs to a Mrs Sawyer.' Why, sure, said Aunt El, that's Mrs Sawyer's, right there across the street. The only boarding house around here, it is an old tall dark place with about two dozen lightning rods scattered on the roof: Mrs Sawyer is scared to death in a thunderstorm.

Colouring like an apple, Billy Bob said, please, ma'am, it being such a hot day and all, wouldn't they rest a spell and have some tutti-frutti? and Aunt El said yes, by all means, but Miss Bobbit shook her head. 'Very fattening, tutti-frutti; but *merci* you kindly,' and they started across the road, the mother half-dragging her parcels in the dust. Then, and with an earnest expression, Miss Bobbit turned back; the sunflower yellow of her eyes darkened, and she rolled them slightly sideways, as if trying to remember a poem. 'My mother has a disorder of the tongue, so it is necessary that I speak for her,' she announced rapidly and heaved a sigh. 'My mother is a very fine seamstress;

she has made dresses for the society of many cities and towns, including Memphis and Tallahassee. No doubt you have noticed and admired the dress I am wearing. Every stitch of it was handsewn by my mother. My mother can copy any pattern, and just recently she won a twenty-five-dollar prize from the *Ladies' Home Journal*. My mother can also crochet, knit and embroider. If you want any kind of sewing done, please come to my mother. Please advise your friends and family. Thank you.' And then, with a rustle and a swish, she was gone.

Cora McCall and the girls pulled their hair-ribbons nervously, suspiciously, and looked very put out and prune-faced. I'm *Miss* Bobbit, said Cora, twisting her face into an evil imitation, and I'm Princess Elizabeth, that's who I am, ha, ha, ha. Furthermore, said Cora, that dress was just as tacky as could be; personally, Cora said, all my clothes come from Atlanta; plus a pair of shoes from New York, which is not even to mention my silver turquoise ring all the way from Mexico City, Mexico. Aunt El said they ought not to behave that way about a fellow child, a stranger in the town, but the girls went on like a huddle of witches, and certain boys, the sillier ones that liked to be with the girls, joined in and said things that made Aunt El go red and declare she was going to send them all home and tell their daddies, to boot. But before she could carry forward this threat Miss Bobbit herself intervened by traipsing across the Sawyer porch, costumed in a new and startling manner.

The older boys, like Billy Bob and Preacher Star, who had sat quietly while the girls razzed Miss Bobbit, and who had watched the house into which she'd disappeared with misty, ambitious faces, they now straightened up and ambled down to the gate. Cora McCall sniffed and poked out her lower lip, but the rest of us went and sat on the steps. Miss Bobbit paid us no mind whatever. The Sawyer yard is dark with mulberry trees and it is planted with grass and sweet shrub. Sometimes after a rain you can smell the sweet shrub all the way into our house; and in the centre of this yard there is a sundial which Mrs Sawyer installed in 1912 as a memorial to her Boston bull, Sunny, who died after having lapped up a bucket of paint.

Miss Bobbit pranced into the yard toting the victrola, which she put on the sundial; she wound it up, and started a record playing, and it played the Count of Luxembourg. By now it was almost nightfall, a firefly hour, blue as milkglass; and birds like arrows swooped together and swept into the folds of trees. Before storms, leaves and flowers appear to burn with a private light, colour, and Miss Bobbit, got up in a little white skirt like a powder-puff and with strips of gold-glittering tinsel ribboning her hair, seemed set against the darkening all around, to contain this illuminated quality. She held her arms arched over her head, her hands lily-limp, and stood straight up on the tips of her toes. She stood that way for a good long while, and Aunt El said it was right smart of her. Then she began to waltz around and around, and around and around she went until Aunt El said, why, she was plain dizzy from the sight. She stopped only when it was time to re-wind the victrola; and when the moon came rolling down the ridge, and the last supper bell had sounded, and all the children had gone home, and the night iris was beginning to bloom, Miss Bobbit was still there in the dark turning like a top.

We did not see her again for some time. Preacher Star came every morning to our house and stayed straight through to supper. Preacher is a rail-thin boy with a butchy shock of red hair; he has eleven brothers and sisters, and even they are afraid of him, for he has a terrible temper, and is famous in these parts for his green-eyed meanness: last fourth of July he whipped Ollie Overton so bad that Ollie's family had to send him to the hospital in Pensacola, and there was another time he bit off half a mule's ear, chewed it and spit it on the ground. Before Billy Bob got his growth, Preacher played the devil with him, too. He used to drop cockleburrs down his collar, and rub pepper in his eyes, and tear up his homework. But now they are the biggest friends in town: talk alike, walk alike; and occasionally they disappear together for whole days, Lord knows where to. But during these days when Miss Bobbit did not appear they stayed close to the house. They would stand around in the yard trying to slingshot sparrows off telephone poles, or sometimes Billy Bob would play his ukulele, and they would sing so loud Uncle Billy Bob, who is Judge for this county, claimed he could hear them all the way to the courthouse: *send me a letter, send it by mail, send it in care of the Birmingham jail.* Miss Bobbit did not hear them; at least she never poked her head out the door. Then one day Mrs Sawyer, coming over to borrow a cup of sugar, rattled on a good deal about her new boarders. You know she said, squinting her chicken-bright eyes, the husband was a crook, uh huh, the child told me herself. Hasn't an ounce of shame, not a mite. Said her daddy was the dearest daddy and the sweetest singing man in the whole of Tennessee. . . . And I said, honey, where is he? and just as offhand as you please she says, Oh, he's in the penitentiary and we don't hear from him no more. Say, now, does that make your blood run cold? Uh huh, and I been thinking, her mama, I been thinking she's some kinda foreigner: never says a word, and sometimes it looks like she don't understand what nobody says to her. And you know, they eat everything *raw. Raw eggs, raw turnips, carrots –* no meat whatsoever. For reasons of health, the child says, but ho! she's been straight out on the bed running a fever since last Tuesday.

That same afternoon Aunt El went out to water her roses, only to discover them gone. These were special roses, ones she'd planned to send to the flower show in Mobile, and so naturally she got a little hysterical. She rang up the Sheriff, and said, listen here, Sheriff, you come over here right fast. I mean somebody's got off with all my Lady Anne's that I've devoted myself to heart and soul since early spring. When the Sheriff's car pulled up outside our house, all the neighbours along the street came out on their porches, and Mrs Sawyer, layers of cold cream whitening her face, trotted across the road. Oh shoot, she said, very disappointed to find no one had been murdered, oh shoot, she said, nobody's stole them roses. Your Billy Bob brought them roses over and left them for little Bobbit. Aunt El did not say one word. She just marched over to the peach tree, and cut herself a switch. Ohhh, Billy Bob, she stalked along the street calling his name, and then she found him down at Speedy's garage where he and Preacher were watching Speedy take a motor apart. She simply lifted him by the hair and, switching blueblazes, towed him home. But she couldn't make him say he was sorry and she couldn't make him cry. And when she was finished with him he ran into the back-yard and climbed high into the tower of a pecan tree and swore he wasn't ever going to come down. Then his daddy came home, and it was time to have supper. His daddy stood at the window and called to him: Son, we aren't mad with you, so come down and eat your supper. But Billy Bob wouldn't budge. Aunt El went and leaned against the tree. She spoke in a voice soft as the gathering light. I'm sorry, son, she said, I didn't mean whipping you so hard like that. I've fixed a nice supper, son, potato salad and boiled ham and devilled eggs. Go away, said Billy Bob, I don't want no supper, and I hate you like all-fire. His daddy said he ought not to talk like that to his mother, and she began to cry. She stood there under the tree and cried, raising the hem of her skirt to dab at her eyes. I don't hate you, son. . . . If I don't love you I wouldn't whip you. The pecan leaves began to rattle; Billy Bob slid slowly to the ground, and Aunt El, brushing her fingers through his hair, pulled him against her. Aw, Ma, he said, Aw, Ma.

After supper Billy Bob came and flung himself on the foot of my bed. He smelled all sour and sweet, the way boys do, and I felt very sorry for him, especially because he looked so worried. His eyes were almost shut with worry. You're s'posed to send sick folks flowers, he said righteously. About this time we heard the victrola, a lilting faraway sound, and a night moth flew through the window, drifting in the air delicate as the music. But it was dark now, and we couldn't tell if Miss Bobbit was dancing. Billy Bob, as though he were in pain, doubled up on the bed like a jackknife; but his face was suddenly clear, his grubby boy-eyes twitching like candles. She's so cute, he whispered, she's the cutest dickens I ever saw, gee, to hell with it, I don't care, I'd pick all the roses in China.

Preacher would have picked all the roses in China, too. He was as crazy about her as Billy Bob. But Miss Bobbit did not notice them. The sole communication we had with her was a note to Aunt El thanking her for the flowers. Day after day she sat on her porch, always dressed to beat the band, and doing a piece of embroidery, or combing curls in her hair, or reading a Webster's dictionary – formal, but friendly enough; if you said good-day to her she said good-day to you. Even so, the boys never could seem to get up the nerve to go over and talk with her, and most of the time she simply looked through them, even when they tomcatted up and down the street trying to get her eye. They wrestled, played Tarzan, did foolheaded bicycle tricks. It was a sorry business. A great many girls in town strolled by the Sawyer house two and three times within an hour just on the chance of getting a look. Some of the girls who did this were: Cora McCall, Mary Murphy Jones, Janice Ackerman. Miss Bobbit did not show any interest in them either. Cora would not speak to Billy Bob any more. The same was true with Janice and Preacher. As a matter of fact, Janice wrote Preacher a letter in red ink on lace-trimmed paper in which she told him he was vile beyond all human beings and words, that she considered their engagement broken, that he could have back the stuffed squirrel he'd given her. Preacher, saying he wanted to act nice, stopped her the next time she passed our house, and said, well, hell, she could keep that old squirrel if she wanted to. Afterwards, he couldn't understand why Janice ran away bawling the way she did.

Then one day the boys were being crazier than usual; Billy Bob was sagging around in his daddy's World War khakis, and Preacher, stripped to the waist, had a naked woman drawn on his chest with one of Aunt El's old lipsticks. They looked like perfect fools, but Miss Bobbit, reclining in a swing, merely yawned. It was noon, and there was no one passing in the street, except a coloured girl, baby-fat and sugar-plum shaped, who hummed along carrying a pail of blackberries. But the boys, teasing at her like gnats, joined hands and wouldn't let her go by, not until she paid a tariff. I ain't studyin' no tariff, she said, what kinda tariff you talkin' about, mister? A party in the barn, said Preacher, between clenched teeth, mighty nice party in the barn. And she, with a sulky shrug, said, huh, she intended studyin' no barn parties. Whereupon Billy Bob capsized her berry pail, and when she, with despairing, piglike shrieks, bent down in futile gestures of rescue, Preacher, who can be mean as the devil, gave her behind a kick which sent her sprawling jellylike among the blackberries and the dust. Miss Bobbit came tearing across the road, her finger wagging like a metronome; like a schoolteacher she clapped her hands, stamped her foot, and said: 'It is a well-known fact that gentlemen are put on the face of the earth for the protection of ladies. Do you suppose boys behave this way in towns like Memphis, New York, London, Hollywood or Paris?' The boys hung back, and shoved their hands in their pockets. Miss Bobbit helped the coloured girl to her feet; she dusted her off, dried her eyes, held out a handkerchief and told her to blow. 'A pretty pass,' she said, 'a fine situation when a lady can't walk safely in the public daylight.'

Then the two of them went back and sat on Mrs Sawyer's porch; and for the next year they were never far apart, Miss Bobbit and this baby elephant, whose name was Rosalba Cat. At first, Mrs Sawyer raised a fuss about Rosalba being so much at her house. She told Aunt El that it went against the grain to have a nigger lolling smack there in plain sight on her front porch. But Miss Bobbit had a certain magic, whatever she did she did it with completeness, and so directly, so solemnly, that there was nothing to do but accept it. For instance, the tradespeople in town used to snicker when they called her *Miss* Bobbit; but by and by she was Miss Bobbit, and they gave her stiff little bows as she whirled by spinning her parasol. Miss Bobbit told everyone that Rosalba was her sister, which caused a good many jokes; but like most of her ideas, it gradually seemed natural, and when we would overhear them calling each other Sister Rosalba and Sister Bobbit none of us cracked a smile. But Sister Rosalba and Sister Bobbit did some queer things. There was the business about the dogs. Now there are a great many dogs in this town, rat-terriers, bird-dogs, bloodhounds; they trail along the forlorn noon-hot streets in sleepy herds of six to a dozen, all waiting only for dark and the moon, when straight through the lonesome hours you can hear them howling: someone is dying, someone is dead. Miss Bobbit complained to the Sheriff; she said that certain of the dogs always planted themselves under her window, and that she was a light sleeper to begin with; what is more, and as Sister Rosalba said, she did not believe they were dogs at all, but some kind of devil. Naturally the Sheriff did nothing; and so she took the matter into her own hands. One morning, after an especially loud night, she was seen stalking through the town with Rosalba at her side, Rosalba carrying a flower basket filled with rocks; whenever they saw a dog they paused while Miss Bobbit scrutinized him. Sometimes she would shake her head, but more often she said, 'Yes, that's one of them, Sister Rosalba,' and Sister Rosalba, with ferocious aim, would take a rock from her basket and crack the dog between the eyes.

Another thing that happened concerns Mr Henderson. Mr Henderson has a back room in the Sawyer house; a tough runt of a man who formerly was a wildcat oil prospector in Oklahoma, he is about seventy years old and, like a lot of old men, obsessed by functions of the body. Also, he is a terrible drunk. One time he had been drunk for two weeks; whenever he heard Miss Bobbit and Sister Rosalba moving around the house, he would charge to the top of the stairs and bellow down to Mrs Sawyer that there were midgets in the walls trying to get at his supply of toilet paper. They've already stolen fifteen cents' worth, he said. One evening, when the two girls were sitting under a tree in the yard, Mr Henderson, sporting nothing more than a nightshirt, stamped out after them. Steal all my toilet paper, will you? he hollered, I'll show you midgets. ... Somebody come help me, else these midget bitches are liable to make off with every sheet in town. It was Billy Bob and Preacher who caught Mr Henderson and held him until some grown men arrived and began to tie him up. Miss Bobbit, who had behaved with admirable calm, told the men they did not know how to tie a proper knot, and undertook to do so herself. She did such a good job that all the circulation stopped in Mr Henderson's hands and feet and it was a month before he could walk again.

It was shortly afterwards that Miss Bobbit paid us a call.

She came on Sunday and I was there alone, the family having gone to church. 'The odours of a church are so offensive,' she said, leaning forward and with her hands folded primly before her. 'I don't want you to think I'm a heathen, Mr C.; I've had enough experience to know that there is a God and that there is a Devil. But the way to tame the Devil is not to go down there to church and listen to what a sinful mean fool he is. No, love the Devil like you do Jesus: because he is a powerful man, and will do you a good turn if he knows you trust him. He has frequently done me good turns, like at dancing school in Memphis. ... I always called in the Devil to help me get the biggest part in our annual show. That is common sense; you see, I knew Jesus wouldn't have any truck with dancing. Now, as a matter of fact, I have called in the Devil just recently. He is the only one who can help me get out of this town. Not that I live here, not exactly. I think always about somewhere else, somewhere else where everything is dancing, like people dancing in the streets, and everything is pretty, like children on their birthdays. My precious papa said I live in the sky, but if he'd lived more in the sky he'd be rich like he wanted to be. The trouble with my papa was he did not love the Devil, he let the Devil love him. But I am very smart in that respect; I know the next best thing is very often the best. It was the next best thing for us to move to this town; and since I can't pursue my career here, the next best thing for me is to start a little business on the side. Which is what I have done. I am sole subscription agent in this county for an impressive list of magazines, including *Reader's Digest*, *Popular Mechanics*, *Dime Detective* and *Child's Life*. To be sure, Mr C., I'm not here to sell you anything. But I have a thought in mind. I was thinking those two boys that are always hanging around here, it occurred to me that they are men, after all. Do you suppose they would make a pair of likely assistants?'

Billy Bob and Preacher worked hard for Miss Bobbit, and for Sister Rosalba, too. Sister Rosalba carried a line of cosmetics called Dewdrop, and it was part of the boys' job to deliver purchases to her customers. Billy Bob used to be so tired in the evening he could hardly chew his supper. Aunt El said it

35

was a shame and a pity, and finally one day when Billy Bob came down with a touch of sunstroke she said, all right, that settled it, Billy Bob would just have to quit Miss Bobbit. But Billy Bob cursed her out until his daddy had to lock him in his room; whereupon he said he was going to kill himself. Some cook we'd had told him once that if you ate a mess of collards all slopped over with molasses it would kill you sure as shooting; and so that is what he did. I'm dying, he said, rolling back and forth on his bed, I'm dying and nobody cares.

Miss Bobbit came over and told him to hush up. 'There's nothing wrong with you, boy,' she said. 'All you've got is a stomach ache.' Then she did something that shocked Aunt El very much: she stripped the covers off Billy Bob and rubbed him down with alcohol from head to toe. When Aunt El told her she did not think that was a nice thing for a little girl to do, Miss Bobbit replied: 'I don't know whether it's nice or not, but it's certainly very refreshing.' After which Aunt El did all she could to keep Billy Bob from going back to work for her, but his daddy said to leave him alone, they would have to let the boy lead his own life.

Miss Bobbit was very honest about money. She paid Billy Bob and Preacher their exact commission and she never let them treat her, as they often tried to do, at the drugstore or to the picture-show. 'You'd better save your money,' she told them. 'That is, if you want to go to college. Because neither one of you has got the brains to win a scholarship, not even a football scholarship.' But it was over money that Billy Bob and Preacher had a big falling out; that was not the real reason, of course: the real reason was that they had grown cross-eyed jealous over Miss Bobbit. So one day, and he had the gall to do this right in front of Billy Bob, Preacher said to Miss Bobbit that she'd better check her accounts carefully because he had more than a suspicion that Billy Bob wasn't turning over to her *all* the money he collected. That's a damned lie, said Billy Bob, and with a clean left hook he knocked Preacher off the Sawyer porch and jumped after him into a bed of nasturtiums. But once Preacher got a hold on him, Billy Bob didn't stand a chance. Preacher even rubbed dirt in his eyes. During all this, Mrs Sawyer, leaning out an upper-storey window, screamed like an eagle, and Sister Rosalba, fatly cheerful, ambiguously shouted, Kill him! Kill him! Kill him! Only Miss Bobbit seemed to know what she was doing. She plugged in the lawn hose, and gave the boys a closeup, blinding bath. Gasping, Preacher staggered to his feet. Oh, honey, he said, shaking himself like a wet dog, honey, you've got to decide. 'Decide *what*?' said Miss Bobbit, right away in a huff. Oh, honey, wheezed Preacher, you don't want us boys killing each other. You got to decide who is your real true sweetheart. 'Sweetheart, my eye,' said Miss Bobbit. 'I should've known better than to get myself involved with a lot of country children. What sort of businessman are you going to make? Now, you listen here, Preacher Star: I don't want a sweetheart, and if I did, it wouldn't be you. As a matter of fact, you don't even get up when a lady enters the room.'

Preacher spit on the ground and swaggered over to Billy Bob. Come on, he said, just as though nothing had happened, she's a hard one, she is, she don't want nothing but to make trouble between two good friends. For a moment it looked as if Billy Bob was going to join him in a peaceful togetherness; but suddenly, coming to his senses, he drew back and made a gesture. The boys regarded each other a full minute, all the closeness between them turning an ugly colour: you can't hate so much unless you love, too. And Preacher's face showed all of this. But there was nothing for him to do except go away. Oh, yes, Preacher, you looked so lost that day that for the first time I really liked you, so skinny and mean and lost going down the road all by yourself.

They did not make it up, Preacher and Billy Bob; and it was not because they didn't want to, it was only that there did not seem to be any straight way for their friendship to happen again. But they couldn't get rid of this friendship: each was always aware of what the other was up to; and when Preacher found himself a new buddy, Billy Bob moped around for days, picking things up, dropping them again, or doing sudden wild things, like purposely poking his finger in the electric fan. Some times in the evenings Preacher would pause by the gate and talk with Aunt El. It was only to torment Billy Bob, I suppose, but he stayed friendly with all of us, and at Christmas time he gave us a huge box of shelled peanuts. He left a present for Billy Bob, too. It turned out to be a book of Sherlock Holmes; and on the flyleaf there was scribbled, 'Friends Like Ivy On The Wall Must Fall.' That's the corniest thing I ever saw, Billy Bob said. Jesus, what a dope he is! But then, and though it was a cold winter day, he went in the backyard and climbed up into the pecan tree, crouching there all afternoon in the blue December branches.

But most of the time he was happy, because Miss Bobbit was there, and she was always sweet to him now. She and Sister Rosalba treated him like a man; that is to say, they allowed him to do everything for them. On the other hand, they let him win at three-handed bridge, they never questioned his lies, nor discouraged his ambitions. It was a happy while. However, trouble started again when school began. Miss Bobbit refused to go. 'It's ridiculous,' she said, when one day the principal, Mr Copland, came around to investigate, 'really ridiculous; I can read and write and there are *some* people in this town who have every reason to know that I can count money. No, Mr Copland, consider for a moment and you will see neither of us has the time nor energy. After all, it would only be a matter of whose spirit broke first, yours or mine. And besides, what is there for you to teach me? Now, if you knew anything about dancing, that would be another matter; but under the circumstances, yes, Mr Copland, under the circumstances, I suggest we forget the whole thing.' Mr Copland was perfectly willing to. But the rest of the town thought she ought to be whipped. Horace Deasley wrote a piece in the paper which was titled 'A Tragic Situation'. It was, in his opinion, a tragic situation when a small girl could defy what he, for some reason, termed the Constitution of the United States. The article ended with a question: *Can she get away with it?* She did; and so did Sister Rosalba. Only she was coloured, so no one cared. Billy Bob was not as lucky. It was school for him, all right; but he might as well have stayed home for all the good it did him. On his first report card he got three Fs, a record of some sort. But he is a smart boy. I guess he just couldn't live through those hours without Miss Bobbit; away from her he always seemed half-asleep. He was always in a fight, too; either his eye was black, or his lip was split, or his walk had a limp. He never talked about these fights, but Miss Bobbit was shrewd enough to guess the reason why. 'You are a dear, I know. And I appreciate you, Billy Bob. Only don't fight with people because of me. Of course they say mean things about me. But do you know why that is, Billy Bob? It's a compliment, kind of. Because deep down they think I'm absolutely wonderful.'

And she was right: if you are not admired no one will take the trouble to disapprove. But actually we had no idea of how wonderful she was until there appeared the man known as Manny Fox. This happened late in February. The first news we had of Manny Fox was a series of jovial placards posted up in the stores around town: Manny Fox Presents the Fan Dancer Without the Fan; then, in smaller print: Also, Sensational Amateur Programme Featuring Your Own Neighbours – First Prize, A Genuine Hollywood Screen Test. All this was to take place the following Thursday. The tickets were priced at one dollar each, which around here is a lot of money; but it is not often that we get any kind of flesh entertainment, so everybody shelled out their money and made a great to-do over the whole thing. The drugstore cowboys talked dirty all week, mostly about the tan dancer without the fan, who turned out to be Mrs Manny Fox. They stayed down the highway at the Chucklewood Tourist Camp; but they were in town all day, driving around in an old Packard which had Manny Fox's full name stencilled on all four doors. His wife was a deadpan pimento-tongued redhead with wet lips and moist eyelids; she was quite large actually, but compared to Manny Fox she seemed rather frail, for he was a fat cigar of a man.

They made the pool hall their headquarters, and every afternoon you could find them there, drinking beer and joking with the town loafs. As it developed, Manny Fox's business affairs were not restricted to theatrics. He also ran a kind of employment bureau: slowly he let it be known that for a fee of $150 he could get for any adventurous boys in the county high-class jobs working on fruit ships sailing from New Orleans to South America. The chance of a lifetime, he called it. There are not two boys around here who readily lay their hands on so much as five dollars; nevertheless, a good dozen managed to raise the money. Ada Willingham took all she'd saved to buy an angel tombstone for her husband and gave it to her son, and Acey Trump's papa sold an option on his cotton crop.

But the night of the show! That was a night when all was forgotten: mortgages, and the dishes in the kitchen sink. Aunt El said you'd think we were going to the opera, everybody so dressed up, so pink and sweet-smelling. The Odeon had not been so full since the night they gave away the matched set of sterling silver. Practically everybody had a relative in the show, so there was a lot of nervousness to contend with. Miss Bobbit was the only contestant we knew real well. Billy Bob couldn't sit still; he kept telling us over and over that we mustn't applaud for anybody but Miss Bobbit; Aunt El said that would be very rude, which sent Billy Bob off into a state again; and when his father bought us all bags of popcorn he wouldn't touch his because it would make his hands greasy, and please, another thing, we mustn't be noisy and eat ours while Miss Bobbit was performing. That she was to be a contestant had come as a last-minute surprise. It was logical enough, and there were signs that should've told us; the fact, for instance, that she had not set foot outside the Sawyer house in how many days? And the victrola going half the night, her shadow whirling on the window-shade, and the secret, stuffed look on Sister Rosalba's face whenever asked after Sister Bobbit's health. So there was her name on the programme, listed second, in fact, though she did not appear for a long while. First came Manny Fox, greased and leering, who told a lot of peculiar jokes, clapping his hands, ha, ha. Aunt El said if he told another joke like that she was going to walk straight out: he did, and she didn't. Before Miss Bobbit came on there were eleven contestants, including Eustacia Bernstein, who imitated movie stars so that they all sounded like Eustacia, and there was an extraordinary Mr Buster Riley, a jug-eared old wool-hat from way in the back country who played 'Waltzing Matilda' on a saw. Up to that point, he was the hit of the show; not that there was any marked difference in the various receptions, for everybody applauded generously, everybody, that is, except Preacher Star. He was sitting two rows ahead of us, greeting each act with a donkey-loud boo. Aunt El said she was never going to speak to him again. The only person he ever applauded was Miss Bobbit. No doubt the Devil was on her side, but she deserved it. Out she came, tossing her hips, her curls, rolling her eyes. You could tell right away it wasn't going to be one of her classical numbers. She tapped across the stage, daintily holding up the sides of a cloud-blue skirt. That's the cutest thing I ever saw, said Billy Bob, smacking his thigh, and Aunt El had to agree that Miss Bobbit looked real sweet. When she started to twirl the whole audience broke into spontaneous applause; so she did it all over again, hissing, 'Faster, faster,' at poor Miss Adelaide, who was at the piano doing her Sunday-school best. 'I was born in China, and raised in Jay-pan . . .' We had never heard her sing before, and she had a rowdy sand-paper voice. '. . . if you don't like my peaches, stay away from my can, o-ho o-ho!' Aunt El gasped; she gasped again when Miss Bobbit, with a bump, up-ended her skirt to display blue-lace underwear, thereby collecting most of the whistles the boys had been saving for the fan dancer without the fan, which was just as well, as it later turned out, for that lady, to the tune of 'An apple for the Teacher' and cries of gyp gyp, did her routine attired in a bathing suit. But showing off her bottom was not Miss Bobbit's final triumph. Miss Adelaide commenced an ominous thundering in the darker keys, at which point Sister Rosalba, carrying a lighted Roman candle, rushed on-stage and handed it to Miss Bobbit, who was in the midst of a full split; she made it, too, and just as she did the Roman candle burst into fiery balls of red, white and blue, and we all had to stand up because she was singing 'The Star Spangled Banner' at the top of her lungs. Aunt El said afterwards that it was one of the most gorgeous things she'd ever seen on the American stage.

Well, she surely did deserve a Hollywood screen test and, inasmuch as she won the contest, it looked as though she were going to get it. Manny Fox said she was: honey, he said, you're real star stuff. Only he skipped town the next day, leaving nothing but hearty promises. Watch the mails, my friends, you'll all be hearing from me. That is what he said to the boys whose money he'd taken, and that is what he said to Miss Bobbit. There are three deliveries daily, and this sizeable group gathered at the post office for all of them, a jolly crowd growing gradually joyless. How their hands trembled when a letter slid into their mailbox. A terrible hush came over them as the days passed. They all knew what the other was thinking, but no one could bring himself to say it, not even Miss Bobbit. Postmistress Patterson said it plainly, however: the man's a crook, she said, I knew he was a crook to begin with, and if I have to look at your faces one more day I'll shoot myself.

Finally, at the end of two weeks, it was Miss Bobbit who broke the spell. Her eyes had grown more vacant than anyone had ever supposed they might, but one day, after the last mail was up, all her old sizzle came back. 'O.K., boys, it's lynch law now,' she said, and proceeded to herd the whole troupe home with her. This was the first meeting of the Manny Fox Hangman's Club, an organization which, in a more social form, endures to this day, though Manny Fox has long since been caught and, so to say, hung. Credit for this went quite properly to Miss Bobbit. Within a week she'd written over three hundred descriptions of Manny Fox and dispatched them to sheriffs throughout the South; she also wrote letters to papers in the larger cities, and these attracted wide attention. As a result, four of the robbed boys were offered good-paying jobs by the United Fruit Company, and late this spring, when Manny Fox was arrested in Uphigh, Arkansas, where he was pulling the same old dodge, Miss Bobbit was presented with a Good Deed Merit award from the Sunbeam Girls of America. For some reason, she made a point of letting the world know that this did not exactly thrill her. 'I do not approve of the organization,' she said. 'All that rowdy bugle blowing. It's neither good-hearted nor truly feminine. And anyway, what is a good deed? Don't let anybody fool you, a good deed is something you do because you want something in return.' It would be reassuring to report she was wrong, and that her just reward, when at last it came, was given out of kindness and love. However, this is not the case. About a week ago the boys involved in the swindle all received from Manny Fox cheques covering their losses, and Miss Bobbit, with clodhopping determination, stalked into a meeting of the Hangman's Club, which is now an excuse for drinking beer and playing poker every Thursday night. 'Look, boys,' she said, laying it on the line, 'none of you ever thought to see that money again, but now that you have, you ought to invest it in something practical – like me.' The proposition was that they should pool their money and finance her trip to Hollywood; in return, they would get ten per cent of her life's earnings which, after she was a star, and that would not be very long, would make them all rich men. 'At least,' as she said, 'in this part of the country.' Not one of the boys wanted to do it: but when Miss Bobbit looked at you, what was there to say?

Since Monday, it has been raining buoyant summer rain shot through with sun, but dark at night and full of sound, full of dripping leaves, watery chimneys, sleepless scuttlings. Billy Bob is wide-awake, dry-eyed, though everything he does is a little frozen and his tongue is as stiff as a bell tongue. It has not been easy for him, Miss Bobbit's going. Because she'd meant more than that. Than what? Than being thirteen years old and crazy in love. She was the queer things in him, like the pecan tree and liking books and caring enough about people to let them hurt him. She was the things he was afraid to show anyone else. And in the dark the music trickled through the rain: won't there be nights when we will hear it just as though it were really there? And afternoons when the shadows will be all at once confused, and she will pass before us, unfurling across the lawn like a pretty piece of ribbon? She laughed to Billy Bob; she held his hand, she even kissed him. 'I'm not going to die,' she said. 'You'll come out there, and we'll climb a mountain, and we'll all live there together, you and me and Sister Rosalba.' But Billy Bob knew it would never happen that way, and so when the music came through the dark he would stuff the pillow over his head.

Only there was a strange smile about yesterday, and that was the day she was leaving. Around noon the sun came out, bringing with it into the air all the sweetness of wisteria. Aunt El's yellow Lady Anne's were blooming again, and she did something wonderful, she told Billy Bob he could pick them and give them to Miss Bobbit for good-bye. All afternoon Miss Bobbit sat on the porch surrounded by people who stopped by to wish her well. She looked as though she were going to Communion, dressed in white and with a white parasol. Sister Rosalba had given her a handkerchief, but she had to borrow it back because she couldn't stop blubbering. Another little girl brought a baked chicken, presumably to be eaten on the bus; the only trouble was she'd forgotten to take out the insides before cooking it. Miss Bobbit's mother said that was all right by her, chicken was chicken, which is memorable because it is the single opinion she ever voiced. There was only one sour note. For hours Preacher Star had been hanging around down at the corner, sometimes standing at the kerb tossing a coin, and sometimes hiding behind a tree, as if he didn't want anyone to see him. It made everybody nervous. About twenty minutes before bus time he sauntered up and leaned against our gate. Billy Bob was still in the garden picking roses; by now he had enough for a bonfire, and their smell was as heavy as wind. Preacher stared at him until he lifted his head. As they looked at each other the rain began again, falling fine as sea spray and coloured by a rainbow. Without a word, Preacher went over and started helping Billy Bob separate the roses into two giant bouquets: together they carried them to the kerb. Across the street there were bumblebees of talk, but when Miss Bobbit saw them, two boys whose flower-masked faces were like yellow moons, she rushed down the steps, her arms outstretched. You could see what was going to happen;

and we called out, our voices like lightning in the rain, but Miss Bobbit, running toward those moons of roses, did not seem to hear. That is when the six o'clock bus ran over her.

Shut a Final Door

'Walter, listen to me: if everyone dislikes you, works against you, don't believe they do so arbitrarily; you create these situations for yourself.'

Anna had said that, and, though his healthier side told him she intended nothing malicious (if Anna was not a friend, then who was?), he'd despised her for it, had gone around telling everybody how much he despised Anna, what a bitch she was. That woman! he said, don't trust that Anna. This plain-spoken act of hers – nothing but a cover-up for all her repressed hostility; terrible liar, too, can't believe a word she says: dangerous, my God! And naturally all he said went back to Anna, so that when he called about a play-opening they'd planned attending together she told him. 'Sorry, Walter, I can't afford you any longer. I understand you very well, and I have a certain amount of sympathy. It's very compulsive, your malice, and you aren't too much to blame, but I don't want ever to see you again because I'm not so well myself that I can afford it.' But why? And what had he done? Well, sure, he'd gossiped about her, but it wasn't as though he'd meant it, and after all, as he said to Jimmy Bergman (now there was a two-face if ever there was one), what was the use of having friends if you couldn't discuss them objectively?

He said you said they said we said round and round. Round and round, like the paddle-bladed ceiling-fan wheeling above; turning and turning, stirring stale air ineffectively, it made a watch-tick sound, counted seconds in the silence. Walter inched into a cooler part of the bed and closed his eyes against the dark little room. At seven that evening he'd arrived in New Orleans, at seven-thirty he'd registered in this hotel, an anonymous, sidestreet place. It was August, and it was as though bonfires burned in the red night sky, and the unnatural Southern landscape, observed so assiduously from the train, and which, trying to sublimate all else, he retraced in memory, intensified a feeling of having travelled to the end, the falling off.

But why he was here in this stifling hotel in this faraway town he could not say. There was a window in the room, but he could not seem to get it open, and he was afraid to call the bellboy (what queer eyes that kid had!), and he was afraid to leave the hotel, for what if he got lost? and if he got lost, even a little, then he would be lost altogether. He was hungry; he hadn't eaten since breakfast, so he found some peanut-butter crackers left over from a package he'd bought in Saratoga, and washed them down with a finger of Four Roses, the last. It made him sick. He vomited in the wastebasket, collapsed back on the bed, and cried until the pillow was wet. After a while he just lay there in the hot room, shivering, just lay there and watched the slow-turning fan; there was no beginning to its action, and no end; it was a circle.

An eye, the earth, the rings of a tree, everything is a circle and all circles, Walter said, have a centre. It was crazy for Anna to say what had happened was his own doing. If there was anything wrong with him really, then it had been made so by circumstances beyond his control, by, say, his churchly mother, or his father, an insurance official in Hartford, or his older sister, Cecile, who'd married a man forty years her senior. 'I just wanted to get out of the house.' That was her excuse, and, to tell the truth, Walter had thought it reasonable enough.

But he did not know where to begin thinking about himself, did not know where to find the centre. The first telephone call? No, that had been only three days ago and, properly speaking, was the end, not the beginning. Well, he could start with Irving, for Irving was the first person he'd known in New York.

Now Irving was a sweet little Jewish boy with a remarkable talent for chess and not much else: he had silky hair, and pink baby cheeks, and looked about sixteen. Actually he was twenty-three, Walter's age, and they'd met at a bar in the Village. Walter was alone and very lonesome in New York, and so when this sweet little Irving was friendly he decided maybe it would be a good idea to be friendly, too – because you never can tell. Irving knew a great many people, and everyone was very fond of him, and he introduced Walter to all his friends.

And there was Margaret. Margaret was more or less Irving's girl friend. She was only so-so looking (her eyes bulged, there was always a little lipstick on her teeth, she dressed like a child of ten), but she had a hectic brightness which Walter found attractive. He could not understand why she bothered with Irving at all. 'Why do you?' he said, on one of the long walks they'd begun taking together in Central Park.

'Irving is sweet,' she said, 'and he loves me very purely, and who knows: I might just as well marry him.'

'A damn fool thing to do,' he said. 'Irving could never be your husband because he's really your little brother. Irving is everyone's little brother.'

Margaret was too bright not to see the truth in this. So one day when Walter asked if he might not make love to her she said, all right, she didn't mind if he did. They made love often after that.

Eventually Irving heard about it, and one Monday there was a nasty scene in, curiously enough, the same bar where they'd met. There had been that evening a party in honour of Kurt Kuhnhardt (Kuhnhardt Advertising), Margaret's boss, and she and Walter had gone together, afterwards stopping by this bar for a nightcap. Except for Irving and a couple of girls in slacks the place was empty. Irving was sitting at the bar, his cheeks quite pink, his eyes rather glazed. He looked like a little boy playing grownup, for his legs were too short to reach the stool's footrest; they dangled doll-like. The instant Margaret recognized him she tried to turn around and walk out, but Walter wouldn't let her. And anyway, Irving had seen them: never taking his eyes from them, he put down his whiskey, slowly climbed off the stool, and, with a kind of sad, ersatz toughness, strutted forward.

'Irving, dear,' said Margaret, and stopped, for he'd given her a terrible look.

His chin was trembling. 'You go away,' he said, and it was

as though he were denouncing some childhood tormentor, 'I
hate you.' Then, almost in slow motion, he swung out and, as
if he clutched a knife, struck Walter's chest. It was not much
of a blow, and when Walter did nothing but smile, Irving
slumped against a jukebox, screaming: 'Fight me, you damned
coward; come on, and I'll kill you, I swear before God I will.'
So that was how they left him.

Walking home, Margaret began to cry in a soft tired way.
'He'll never be sweet again,' she said.

And Walter said, 'I don't know what you mean.'

'Oh, yes, you do,' she told him, her voice a whisper. 'Yes,
you do; the two of us, we've taught him how to hate. Somehow
I don't think he ever knew before.'

Walter had been in New York now four months. His origin-
al capital of five hundred dollars had fallen to fifteen, and
Margaret lent him money to pay his January rent at the Bre-
voort. Why, she wanted to know, didn't he move to some place
cheaper? Well, he told her, it was better to have a good address.
And what about a job? When was he going to start working?
Or was he? Sure, he said, sure, as a matter of fact he thought
about it a good deal. But he didn't intend fooling around with
just any little jerkwater thing that came along. He wanted
something good, something with a future, something in, say,
advertising. All right, said Margaret, maybe she could help
him; at any rate, she'd speak with her boss, Mr Kuhnhardt.

2

The K.K.A., so called, was a middle-sized agency, but, as such
things go, very good, the best. Kurt Kuhnhardt, who'd found-
ed it in 1925, was a curious man with a curious reputation: a
lean, fastidious German, a bachelor, he lived in an elegant
black house on Sutton Place, a house interestingly furnished
with, among other things, three Picassos, a superb musicbox,
South Sea Island masks, and a burly Danish youngster, the
houseboy. He invited occasionally some one of his staff in to
dinner, whoever was favourite at the moment, for he was
continually selecting protégés. It was a dangerous position,

these alliances being, as they were, whimsical and uncertain: the protégé found himself checking the want ads when, just the evening previous, he'd dined most enjoyably with his benefactor. During his second week at the K.K.A., Walter, who had been hired as Margaret's assistant, received a memorandum from Mr Kuhnhardt asking him to lunch, and this, of course, excited him unspeakably.

'Kill-joy?' said Margaret, straightening his tie, plucking lint off his lapel. 'Nothing of the sort. It's just that – well, Kuhnhardt's wonderful to work for so long as you don't get too involved – or you're likely not to be working – period.'

Walter knew what she was up to; she didn't fool him a minute; he felt like telling her so, too, but restrained himself; it wasn't time yet. One of these days, though, he was going to have to get rid of her, and soon. It was degrading, his working for Margaret. And besides, the tendency from now on would be to keep him down. But nobody could do that, he thought, looking into Mr Kuhnhardt's sea-blue eyes, nobody could keep Walter down.

'You're an idiot,' Margaret told him. 'My God, I've seen these little friendships of K.K.'s a dozen times, and they don't mean a damn. He used to palsy-walsy around with the switchboard operator. All K.K. wants is someone to play the fool. Take my word, Walter, there aren't any short cuts: what matters is how you do your job.'

He said: 'And have you complaints on that score? I'm doing as well as could be expected.'

'It depends on what you mean by expected,' she said.

One Saturday not long afterwards he made a date to meet her in Grand Central. They were going up to Hartford to spend the afternoon with his family, and for this she'd bought a new dress, new hat, and shoes. But he did not show up. Instead, he drove out on Long Island with Mr Kuhnhardt, and was the most awed of three hundred guests at Rosa Cooper's début ball. Rosa Cooper (née Kuppermann) was heiress to the Cooper Dairy Products: a dark, plump, pleasant child with an unnatural British accent, the result of four years at Miss Jewett's. She wrote a letter to a friend named Anna Stimson, who subsequently showed it to Walter: 'Met the divinest man. Danced with him six times, a divine dancer. He is an Advertising Executive, and is terribly divinely good-looking. We have a date – dinner and the theatre!'

Margaret did not mention the episode, nor did Walter. It was as though nothing had happened, except that now, unless there was office business to discuss, they never spoke, never saw each other. One afternoon, knowing she would not be at home, he went to her apartment and used a passkey given him long ago; there were things he'd left here, clothes, some books, his pipe; rummaging around collecting all this he discovered a photograph of himself scrawled red with lipstick: it gave him for an instant the sensation of falling in a dream. He also came across the only gift he'd ever made her, a bottle of L'Heure Bleue, still unopened. He sat down on the bed, and, smoking a cigarette, stroked his hand over the cool pillow, remembering the way her head had laid there, remembering, too, how they used to lie here Sunday mornings reading the funnies aloud, Barney Google and Dick Tracy and Joe Palooka.

He looked at the radio, a little green box; they'd always made love to music, any kind, jazz, symphonies, choir programmes: it had been their signal, for whenever she'd wanted him, she'd said, 'Shall we listen to the radio, darling?' Anyway, it was finished, and he hated her, and that was what he needed to remember. He found the bottle of perfume again, and put it in his pocket: Rosa might like a surprise.

In the office the next day he stopped by the water cooler and Margaret was standing there. She smiled at him fixedly, and said: 'Well, I didn't know you were a thief.' It was the first overt disclosure of the hostility between them. And suddenly it occurred to Walter he hadn't in all the office a single ally. Kuhnhardt? He could never count on him. And everyone else was an enemy: Jackson, Einstein, Fischer, Porter, Capehart, Ritter, Villa, Byrd. Oh, sure, they were all smart enough not to tell him point-blank not so long as K.K.'s enthusiasm continued.

Well, dislike was at least positive, and the one thing he could not tolerate was vague relations, possibly because his own feelings were so indecisive, ambiguous. He was never certain whether he liked X or not. He needed X's love, but was incapable of loving. He could never be sincere with X, never tell him more than fifty per cent of the truth. On the other hand, it was impossible for him to permit X these same imperfections: somewhere along the line Walter was sure he'd be betrayed. He was afraid of X, terrified. Once in high school he'd plagiarized a poem, and printed it in the school magazine; he could not forget its final line, *All our acts are acts of fear*. And when his teacher caught him, had anything ever seemed to him more unjust?

3

He spent most of the early summer week-ends at Rosa Cooper's Long Island place. The house was, as a rule, well staffed with hearty Yale and Princeton undergraduates, which was irritating, for they were the sort of boys who, around Hartford, made green birds fly in his stomach, and seldom allowed him to meet them on their own ground. As for Rosa herself, she was a darling; everyone said so, even Walter.

But darlings are rarely serious, and Rosa was not serious about Walter. He didn't mind too much. He was able on these week-ends to make a good many contacts: Taylor Ovington, Joyce Randolph (the starlet), E. L. McEvoy, a dozen or so people whose names cast considerable glare in his address book. One evening he went with Anna Stimson to see a film featuring the Randolph girl, and before they were scarcely seated everyone for aisles around knew she was a Friend of his, knew she drank too much, was immoral, and not nearly so pretty as Hollywood made her out to be. Anna told him he was an adolescent female. 'You're a man in only one respect, sweetie,' she said.

It was through Rosa that he'd met Anna Stimson. An editor on a fashion magazine, she was almost six feet tall, wore black suits, affected a monocle, a walking cane, and pounds of jingling Mexican silver. She'd been married twice, once to Buck Strong, the horse-opera idol, and she had a child, a fourteen-year-old son who'd had to be put away in what she called a 'corrective academy'.

'He was a nasty child,' she said. 'He liked to take potshots out the window with a .22, and throw things, and steal from Woolworth's: awful brat, just like you.'

Anna was good to him, though, and in her less depressed, less malevolent moments listened kindly while he groaned out his problems, while he explained why he was the way he was. All his life some cheat had been dealing him the wrong cards. Attributing to Anna every vice but stupidity, he liked to use her as a kind of confessor: there was nothing he could tell her of which she might legitimately disapprove. He would say: 'I've told Kuhnhardt a lot of lies about Margaret; I suppose that's pretty rotten, but she would do the same for me; and anyway my idea is not for him to fire her, but maybe transfer her to the Chicago office.'

Or, 'I was in a bookshop, and a man was standing there and we began talking: a middle-aged man, rather nice, very intelligent. When I went outside he followed, a little ways behind: I crossed the street, he crossed the street, I walked fast, he walked fast. This kept up six or seven blocks, and when I finally figured out what was going on I felt tickled, I felt like kidding him on. So I stopped at the corner and hailed a cab; then I turned around and gave this guy a long, long look, and he came rushing up, all smiles. And I jumped in the cab, and slammed the door and leaned out the window and laughed out loud: the look on his face, it was awful, it was like Christ. I can't forget it. And tell me, Anna, why did I do this crazy thing? It was like paying back all the people who've ever hurt me, but it was something else, too.' He would tell Anna these stories, go home and go to sleep. His dreams were clear blue.

Now the problem of love concerned him, mainly because he did not consider it a problem. Nevertheless, he was conscious of being unloved. This knowledge was like an extra heart beating inside him. But there was no one. Anna, perhaps. Did Anna love him? 'Oh,' said Anna, 'when was anything ever what it seemed to be? Now it's a tadpole, now it's a frog. It looks like gold but you put it on your finger and it leaves a green ring.

Take my second husband: he looked like a nice guy, and turned out to be just another heel. Look around this very room: why, you couldn't burn incense in that fireplace, and those mirrors, they give space, they tell a lie. Nothing, Walter, is ever what it seems to be. Christmas trees are cellophane, and snow is only soap chips. Flying around inside us is something called the Soul, and when you die you're never dead; yes, and when we're alive we're never alive. And so you want to know if I love you? Don't be dumb, Walter, we're not even friends. . . .'

4

Listen, the fan: turning wheels of whisper: he said you said they said we said round and round fast and slow while time recalled itself in endless chatter. Old broken fan breaking silence: August the third the third the third.

August the third, a Friday, and it was there, right in Winchell's column, his own name: 'Big shot Ad exec Walter Ranney and dairy heiress Rosa Cooper are telling intimates to start buying rice.' Walter himself had given the item to a friend of a friend of Winchell's. He showed it to the counter boy at the Whelan's where he ate breakfast. 'That's me,' he said, 'I'm the guy,' and the look on the boy's face was good for his digestion.

It was late when he reached the office that morning, and as he walked down the aisle of desks a small gratifying flurry among the typists preceded him. No one said anything, however. Around eleven, after a pleasant hour of doing nothing but feel exhilarated, he went to the drugstore downstairs for a cup of coffee. Three men from the office, Jackson, Ritter and Byrd, were there, and when Walter came in Jackson poked Byrd, and Byrd poked Ritter, and all of them turned around. 'Whatcha say, big shot?' said Jackson, a pink man prematurely bald, and the other two laughed. Acting as if he hadn't heard, Walter stepped quickly into a phone booth. 'Bastards,' he said, pretending to dial a number. And finally, after waiting a long while for them to leave, he made a real call. 'Rosa, hello, did I wake you up?'

'No.'

'Say, did you see Winchell?'

'Yes.'

Walter laughed. 'Where do you suppose he gets that stuff?'

Silence.

'What's the matter? You sound kind of funny.'

'Do I?'

'Are you mad or something?'

'Just disappointed.'

'About what?'

Silence. And then: 'It was a cheap thing to do, Walter, pretty cheap.'

'I don't know what you mean.'

'Good-bye, Walter.'

On the way out he paid the cashier for a cup of coffee he'd forgotten to have. There was a barbershop in the building. He said he wanted a shave; no – make it a haircut; no – a manicure; and suddenly, seeing himself in the mirror, where his face reflected as pale almost as the barber's bib, he knew he did not know what he wanted. Rosa had been right, he was cheap. He'd always been willing to confess his faults, for, by admitting them, it was as if he made them no longer to exist. He went back upstairs, and sat at his desk, and felt as though he were bleeding inside, and wished very much to believe in God. A pigeon strutted on the ledge outside his window. For some time he watched the shimmering sunlit feathers, the wobbly sedateness of its movements; then, before realizing it, he'd picked up and thrown a glass paperweight: the pigeon climbed calmly upward, the paperweight careened like a giant raindrop; suppose, he thought, listening for a faraway scream, suppose it hits someone, kills them? But there was nothing. Only the ticking fingers of typists, a knocking at the door!

'Hey, Ranney, K. K. wants to see you.'

'I'm sorry,' said Mr Kuhnhardt, doodling with a gold pen. 'And I'll write a letter for you, Walter. Any time.'

Now in the elevator the enemy, all submerging with him, crushed Walter between them; Margaret was there wearing a blue hair-ribbon. She looked at him, and her face was different from other faces, not vacant as theirs were, and sterile: here still was compassion. But as she looked at him, she looked through him, too. This is my dream: he must not allow himself to believe otherwise; and yet under his own arm he carried the dream's contradiction, a manila envelope stuffed with all the personals saved from his desk. When the elevator emptied into the lobby, he knew he must speak with Margaret, ask her to forgive him, beg her protection, but she was slipping swiftly towards an exit, losing herself among the enemy. I love you, he said, running after her, I love you, he said, saying nothing.

'Margaret! Margaret!'

She turned around. The blue hair-ribbon matched her eyes, and her eyes, gazing up at him, softened, became rather friendly. Or pitying.

'Please,' he said, 'I thought we could have a drink together, go over to Benny's, maybe. We used to like Benny's, remember?'

She shook her head. 'I've got a date, and I'm late already.'

'Oh.'

'Yes – well, I'm late,' she said, and began to run. He stood watching as she raced down the street, her ribbon streaming, shining in the darkening summer light. And then she was gone.

His apartment, a one-room walk-up near Gramercy Park, needed an airing, a cleaning, but Walter, after pouring a drink, said to hell with it and stretched out on the couch. What was the use? No matter what you did or how hard you tried, it all came finally to zero; everyday everywhere everyone was being cheated, and who was there to blame? It was strange, though; lying here sipping whiskey in the dusk-greying room he felt calmer than he had for God knows how long. It was like the time he'd failed algebra and felt so relieved, so free: failure was definite, a certainty, and there is always peace in certainties. Now he would leave New York, take a vacation trip; he had a few hundred dollars, enough to last until fall.

And, wondering where he should go, he all at once saw, as if a film had commenced running in his head, silk caps, cherry-coloured and lemon, and little, wise-faced men wearing exquisite polka-dot shirts. Closing his eyes, he was suddenly five years old, and it was delicious remembering the cheers, the hot dogs, his father's big pair of binoculars. Saratoga! Shadows masked his face in the sinking light. He turned on a lamp, fixed another drink, put a rumba record on the phonograph, and began to dance, the soles of his shoes whispering on the carpet: he'd often thought that with a little training he could've been a professional.

Just as the music ended, the telephone rang. He simply stood there, afraid somehow to answer, and the lamplight, the furniture, everything in the room went quite dead. When at last he thought it had stopped, it commenced again; louder, it seemed and more insistent. He tripped over a footstool, picked up the receiver, dropped and recovered it, said: 'Yes?'

Long-distance: a call from some town in Pennsylvania, the name of which he didn't catch. Following a series of spasmic rattlings, a voice, dry and sexless and altogether unlike any he'd ever heard before, came through: 'Hello, Walter.'

'Who is this?'

No answer from the other end, only a sound of strong orderly breathing; the connexion was so good it seemed as though whoever it was was standing beside him with lips pressed against his ear. 'I don't like jokes. Who is this?'

'Oh, you know me, Walter. You've known me a long time.' A click, and nothing.

5

It was night and raining when the train reached Saratoga. He'd slept most of the trip, sweating in the hot dampness of the car, and dreamed of an old castle where only old turkeys lived, and dreamed a dream involving his father, Kurt Kuhnhardt, someone no-faced, Margaret and Rosa, Anna Stimson, and a queer fat lady with diamond eyes. He was standing on a long, deserted street; except for an approaching procession of slow, black, funeral-like cars there was no sign of life. Still, he knew, eyes unseen observed his nakedness from every window, and he hailed frantically the first of the limousines; it stopped and a man, his father, invitingly held open the door. Daddy, he yelled, running forward, and the door slammed shut, mashing off his fingers, and his father, with a great belly-laugh, leaned out of the window to toss an enormous wreath of roses. In the second car was Margaret, in the third the lady with the diamond eyes (wasn't this Miss Casey, his old algebra teacher?), in the fourth Mr Kuhnhardt and a new protégé, the no-faced creature. Each door opened, each closed, all laughed, all threw roses. The procession rolled smoothly away down the silent street. And with a terrible scream Walter fell among the mountain of roses: thorns tore wounds, and a sudden rain, a grey cloudburst, shattered the blooms, and washed pale blood bleeding over the leaves.

By the fixed stare of a woman sitting opposite, he realized at once he'd yelled aloud in his sleep. He smiled at her sheepishly, and she looked away with, he imagined, some embarrassment. She was a cripple; on her left foot she wore a giant shoe. Later, in the Saratoga station, he helped with her luggage, and they shared a taxi; there was no conversation: each sat in his corner looking at the rain, the blurred lights. In New York a few hours before he'd withdrawn from the bank all his savings, locked the door of his apartment, and left no messages; furthermore, there was in this town not a soul who knew him. It was a good feeling.

The hotel was filled: not to mention the racing crowd, there was, the desk clerk told him, a medical convention. No, sorry, he didn't know of a room anywhere. Maybe tomorrow.

So Walter found the bar. As long as he was going to stay up all night he might as well do it drunk. The bar, very large, very hot and noisy, was brilliant with summer-season grotesques: sagging silver-fox ladies, and little stunted jockeys, and pale loud-voiced men wearing cheap fantastic checks. After a couple of drinks, though, the noise seemed far away. Then, glancing around, he saw the cripple. She was alone at a table where she sat primly sipping crème de menthe. They exchanged a smile. Rising, Walter went to join her. 'It's not like we were strangers,' she said, as he sat down. 'Here for the races, I suppose?'

'No,' he said, 'just a rest. And you?'

She pursed her lips. 'Maybe you noticed I've got a clubfoot. Oh, sure now, don't look surprised: you noticed, everybody does. Well, see,' she said, twisting the straw in her glass, 'see, my doctor's going to give a talk at this convention, going to talk about me and my foot on account of I'm pretty special. Gee, I'm scared. I mean I'm going to have to show off my foot.'

Walter said he was sorry, and she said, oh, there was nothing to be sorry about; after all, she was getting a little vacation out of it, wasn't she? 'And I haven't been out of the city in six years. It was six years ago I spent a week at the Bear Mountain Inn.' Her cheeks were red, rather mottled, and her eyes, set too closely together, were lavender-coloured, intense: they seemed never to blink. She wore a gold band on her wedding finger; play-acting, to be sure: it would not have fooled anybody.

'I'm a domestic,' she said, answering a question. 'And there's nothing wrong with that. It's honest and I like it. The people I work for have the cutest kid, Ronnie. I'm better to him than his mother, and he loves me more; he's told me so. That one, she stays drunk all the time.'

It was depressing to listen to, but Walter, afraid suddenly to be alone, stayed and drank and talked in the way he'd once talked to Anna Stimson. Shh! she said at one point, for his voice had risen too high, and a good many people were staring. Walter said the hell with them, he didn't care; it was as if his brain were made of glass, and all the whisky he'd drunk had turned into a hammer; he could feel the shattered pieces rattling in his head, distorting focus, falsifying shape; the cripple, for instance, seemed not one person, but several: Irving, his mother, a man named Bonaparte, Margaret, all those and others: more and more he came to understand experience is a circle of which no moment can be isolated, forgotten.

6

The bar was closing. They went Dutch on the check and, while waiting for change, neither spoke. Watching him with her unblinking lavender eyes, she seemed quite controlled, but there was going on inside, he could tell, some subtle agitation. When the waiter returned they divided the change, and she said: 'If you want to, you can come to my room.' A rash-like blush covered her face. 'I mean, you said you didn't have any place to sleep ...' Walter reached out and took her hand: the smile she gave him was touchingly shy.

Reeking with dime-store perfume, she came out of the bathroom wearing only a sleazy flesh-coloured kimono, and the monstrous black shoe. It was then that he realized he could never go through with it. And he'd never felt so sorry for himself: not even Anna Stimson would ever have forgiven him this. 'Don't look,' she said, and there was a trembling in her voice, 'I'm funny about anybody seeing my foot.'

He turned to the window, where pressing elm leaves rustled in the rain, and lightning, too far off for sound, winked whitely. 'All right,' she said. Walter did not move.

'All right,' she repeated anxiously. 'Shall I put out the light? I mean, maybe you like to get ready – in the dark.'

He came to the edge of the bed, and, bending down, kissed her cheek. 'I think you're so very sweet, but ...'

The telephone interrupted. She looked at him dumbly. 'Jesus God,' she said, and covered the mouthpiece with her hand, 'it's long-distance! I'll bet it's about Ronnie! I'll bet he's sick, or – hello – what? – Ranney? Gee, no. You've got the wrong ...'

'Wait,' said Walter, taking the receiver. 'This is me, this is Walter Ranney.'

'Hello, Walter.'

The voice, dull and sexless and remote, went straight to the pit of his stomach. The room seemed to seesaw, to buckle. A moustache of sweat sprouted on his upper lip. 'Who is this?' he said so slowly the words did not connect coherently.

'Oh, you know me, Walter. You've known me a long time.' Then silence: whoever it was had hung up.

'Gee,' said the woman, 'now how do you suppose they knew you were in my room? I mean – say, was it bad news? You look kind of ...'

Walter fell across her, clutching her to him, pressing his wet cheek against hers. 'Hold me,' he said, discovering he could still cry. 'Hold me, please.'

'Poor little boy,' she said, patting his back. 'My poor little boy: we're awfully alone in this world, aren't we?' And presently he went to sleep in her arms.

But he had not slept since, nor could he now, not even listening to the lazy lull of the fan; in its turning he could hear train wheels: Saratoga to New York, New York to New Orleans. And New Orleans he'd chosen for no special reason, except that it was a town of strangers, and a long way off. Four spinning fan blades, wheels and voices, round and round; and after all, as he saw it now, there was to this network of malice no ending, none whatever.

Water flushed down wall pipes, steps passed overhead, keys jangled in the hall, a news commentator rumbled somewhere beyond, next door a little girl said, why? Why? W H Y? Yet in the room there was a sense of silence. His feet shining in the transom-light looked like amputated stone: the gleaming toenails were ten small mirrors, all reflecting greenly. Sitting up, he rubbed sweat off with a towel; now more than anything the heat frightened him, for it made him know tangibly his own helplessness. He threw the towel across the room, where, landing on a lampshade, it swung back and forth. At this moment the telephone rang. And rang. And it was ringing so loud he was sure all the hotel could hear. An army would be pounding at his door. So he pushed his face into the pillow, covered his ears with his hands, and thought: think of nothing things, think of wind.

Jug of Silver

After school I used to work in the Valhalla drugstore. It was owned by my uncle, Mr Ed Marshall. I call him Mr Marshall because everybody, including his wife, called him Mr Marshall. Nevertheless he was a nice man.

This drugstore was maybe old-fashioned, but it was large and dark and cool: during summer months there was no pleasanter place in town. At the left, as you entered, was a tobacco-magazine counter behind which, as a rule, sat Mr Marshall: a squat, square-faced, pinkfleshed man with looping, manly, white moustaches. Beyond this counter stood the beautiful soda fountain. It was very antique and made of fine, yellowed marble, smooth to the touch but without a trace of cheap glaze. Mr Marshall bought it at an auction in New Orleans in 1910 and was plainly proud of it. When you sat on the high, delicate stools and looked across the fountain you could see yourself reflected softly, as though by candlelight, in a row of ancient, mahogany-framed mirrors. All general merchandise was displayed in glass-doored, curio-like cabinets that were locked with brass keys. There was always in the air the smell of syrup and nutmeg and other delicacies.

The Valhalla was the gathering place of Wachata County till a certain Rufus McPherson came to town and opened a second drugstore directly across the courthouse square. This old Rufus McPherson was a villain; that is, he took away my uncle's trade. He installed fancy equipment such as electric fans and coloured lights; he provided kerb service and made grilled-cheese sandwiches to order. Naturally, though some remained devoted to Mr Marshall, most folks couldn't resist Rufus McPherson.

For a while, Mr Marshall chose to ignore him: if you were

to mention McPherson's name he would sort of snort, finger his moustaches and look the other way. But you could tell he was mad. And getting madder. Then one day towards the middle of October I strolled into the Valhalla to find him sitting at the fountain playing dominoes and drinking wine with Hamurabi.

Hamurabi was an Egyptian and some kind of dentist, though he didn't do much business as the people hereabouts have un-usually strong teeth, due to an element in the water. He spent a great deal of his time loafing around the Valhalla and was my uncle's chief buddy. He was a handsome figure of a man, this Hamurabi, being dark-skinned and nearly seven feet tall; the matrons of the town kept their daughters under lock and key and gave him the eye themselves. He had no foreign accent whatsoever, and it was always my opinion that he wasn't any more Egyptian than the man in the moon.

Anyway, there they were swigging red Italian wine from a gallon jug. It was a troubling sight, for Mr Marshall was a renowned teetotaler. So naturally, I thought: Oh, golly, Rufus McPherson has finally got his goat. That was not the case, however.

'Here, son,' said Mr Marshall, 'come have a glass of wine.'

'Sure,' said Hamurabi, 'help us finish it up. It's store bought, so we can't waste it.'

Much later, when the jug was dry, Mr Marshall picked it up and said, 'Now we shall see!' And with that disappeared out into the afternoon.

'Where's he off to?' I asked.

'Ah,' was all Hamurabi would say. He liked to devil me.

A half-hour passed before my uncle returned. He was stooped and grunting under the load he carried. He set the jug atop the fountain and stepped back, smiling and rubbing his hands together. 'Well, what do you think?'

'Ah,' purred Hamurabi.

'Gee . . .' I said.

It was the same wine jug, God knows, but there was a won-derful difference; for now it was crammed to the brim with nickels and dimes that shone dully through the thick glass.

'Pretty, eh?' said my uncle. 'Had it done over at the First

National. Couldn't get in anything bigger-sized than a nickel. Still, there's lotsa money in there, let me tell you.'

'But what's the point, Mr Marshall?' I said. 'I mean, what's the idea?'

Mr Marshall's smile deepened to a grin. 'This here's a jug of silver, you might say. . . .'

'The pot at the end of the rainbow,' interrupted Hamurabi.

'. . . and the idea, as you call it, is for folks to guess how much money is in there. For instance, say you buy a quarter's worth of stuff – well, then you get to take a chance. The more you buy, the more chances you get. And I'll keep all guesses in a ledger till Christmas Eve, at which time whoever comes closest to the right amount will get the whole shebang.'

Hamurabi nodded solemnly. 'He's playing Santa Claus – a mighty crafty Santa Claus,' he said. 'I'm going home and write a book: *The Skilful Murder of Rufus McPherson*.' To tell the truth, he sometimes did write stories and send them out to magazines. They always came back.

It was surprising, really like a miracle, how Wachata County took to the jug. Why, the Valhalla hadn't done so much business since Station Master Tully, poor soul, went stark raving mad and claimed to have discovered oil back of the depot, causing the town to be overrun with wildcat prospectors. Even the poolhall bums who never spent a cent on anything not connected with whisky or women took to investing their spare cash in milk shakes. A few elderly ladies publicly disapproved of Mr Marshall's enterprise as a kind of gambling, but they didn't start any trouble and some even found occasion to visit us and hazard a guess. The school kids were crazy about the whole thing, and I was very popular because they figured I knew the answer.

'I'll tell you why all this is,' said Hamurabi, lighting one of the Egyptian cigarettes he bought by mail from a concern in New York City. 'It's not for the reason you may imagine; not, in other words, avidity. No. It's the mystery that's enchanting. Now you look at those nickels and dimes and what do you think: ah, so much! No, no. You think: ah, *how* much? And that's a profound question, indeed. It can mean different things to different people. Understand?'

And oh, was Rufus McPherson wild! When you're in trade, you count on Christmas to make up a large share of your yearly profit, and he was hard pressed to find a customer. So he tried to imitate the jug; but being such a stingy man he filled his with pennies. He also wrote a letter to the editor of *The Banner*, our weekly paper, in which he said that Mr Marshall ought to be 'tarred and feathered and strung up for turning innocent little children into confirmed gamblers and sending them down the path to Hell!' You can imagine what kind of laughing stock he was. Nobody had anything for McPherson but scorn. And so by the middle of November he just stood on the sidewalk outside his store and gazed bitterly at the festivities across the square.

At about this time Appleseed and sister made their first appearance.

He was a stranger in town. At least no one could recall ever having seen him before. He said he lived on a farm a mile past Indian Branches; told us his mother weighed only seventy-four pounds and that he had an older brother who would play the fiddle at anybody's wedding for fifty cents. He claimed that Appleseed was the only name he had and that he was twelve years old. But his sister, Middy, said he was eight. His hair was straight and dark yellow. He had a tight, weather-tanned little face with anxious green eyes that had a very wise and knowing look. He was small and puny and high-strung; and he wore always the same outfit: a red sweater, blue denim britches and a pair of man-sized boots that went clop-clop with every step.

It was raining that first time he came into the Valhalla; his hair was plastered round his head like a cap and his boots were caked with red mud from the country roads. Middy trailed behind as he swaggered like a cowboy up to the fountain where I was wiping some glasses.

'I hear you folks got a bottle fulla money you fixin' to give 'way,' he said, looking me square in the eye. 'Seein' as you-all are givin' it away, we'd be obliged iffen you'd give it to us. Name's Appleseed, and this here's my sister, Middy.'

Middy was a sad, sad-looking kid. She was a good bit taller and older-looking than her brother: a regular bean pole. She had tow-coloured hair that was chopped short, and a pale pitiful little face. She wore a faded cotton dress that came way up above her bony knees. There was something wrong with her teeth, and she tried to conceal this by keeping her lips primly pursed like an old lady.

'Sorry,' I said, 'but you'll have to talk with Mr Marshall.'

So sure enough he did. I could hear my uncle explaining what he would have to do to win the jug. Appleseed listened attentively, nodding now and then. Presently he came back and stood in front of the jug and, touching it lightly with his hand, said, 'Ain't it a pretty thing, Middy?'

Middy said, 'Is they gonna give it to us?'

'Naw. What you gotta do, you gotta guess how much money's inside there. And you gotta buy two bits' worth so's even to get a chance.'

'Huh, we ain't got no two bits. Where you 'spec we gonna get us two bits?'

Appleseed frowned and rubbed his chin. 'That'll be the easy part, just leave it to me. The only worrisome thing is: I can't just take a chance and guess. . . . I gotta *know*.'

Well, a few days later they showed up again. Appleseed perched on a stool at the fountain and boldly asked for two glasses of water, one for him and one for Middy. It was on this occasion that he gave out the information about his family: '. . . then there's Papa Daddy, that's my mama's papa, who's a Cajun, an' on accounta that he don't speak English good. My brother, the one what plays the fiddle, he's been in jail three times. . . . It's on accounta him we had to pick up and leave Louisiana. He cut a fella bad in a razor fight over a woman ten years older'n him. She had yellow hair.'

Middy, lingering in the background, said nervously, 'You oughtn't to be tellin' our personal private fam'ly business thataway, Appleseed.'

'Hush now, Middy,' he said, and she hushed. 'She's a good

little gal,' he added, turning to pat her head, 'but you can't let her get away with much. You go look at the picture books, honey, and stop frettin' with your teeth. Appleseed here's got some figurin' to do.'

This figuring meant staring hard at the jug, as if his eyes were trying to eat it up. With his chin cupped in his hand, he studied it for a long period, not batting his eyelids once. 'A lady in Louisiana told me I could see things other folks couldn't see 'cause I was born with a caul on my head.'

'It's a cinch you aren't going to see how much there is,' I told him. 'Why don't you just let a number pop into your head, and maybe that'll be the right one.'

'Uh, uh,' he said, 'too darn risky. Me, I can't take no sucha chance. Now, the way I got it figured, there ain't but one sure-fire thing and that's to count every nickel and dime.'

'Count!'

'Count what?' asked Hamurabi, who had just moseyed inside and was setting himself at the fountain.

'This kid says he's going to count how much is in the jug,' I explained.

Hamurabi looked at Appleseed with interest. 'How do you plan to do that, son?'

'Oh, by countin',' said Appleseed matter-of-factly.

Hamurabi laughed. 'You better have X-ray eyes, son, that's all I can say.'

'Oh, no. All you gotta do is be born with a caul on your head. A lady in Louisiana told me so. She was a witch; she loved me and when my ma wouldn't give me to her she put a hex on her and now my ma don't weigh but seventy-four pounds.'

'Ve-ry in-ter-esting,' was Hamurabi's comment as he gave Appleseed a queer glance.

Middy sauntered up, clutching a copy of *Screen Secrets*. She pointed out a certain photo to Appleseed and said: 'Ain't she the nicest-lookin' lady? Now you see, Appleseed, you see how pretty her teeth are? Not a one outa joint.'

'Well, don't you fret none,' he said.

After they left Hamurabi ordered a bottle of orange Nehi

and drank it slowly, while smoking a cigarette. 'Do you think maybe that kid's O.K. upstairs?' he asked presently in a puzzled voice.

Small towns are best for spending Christmas, I think. They catch the mood quicker and change and come alive under its spell. By the first week in December house doors were decorated with wreaths, and store windows were flashy with red paper bells and snowflakes and glittering isinglass. The kids hiked out into the woods and came back dragging spicy evergreen trees. Already the women were busy baking fruit cakes, unsealing jars of mincemeat and opening bottles of blackberry and scuppernong wine. In the courthouse square a huge tree was trimmed with silver tinsel and coloured electric bulbs that were lighted up at sunset. Late of an afternoon you could hear the choir in the Presbyterian church practising carols for their annual pageant. All over town the japonicas were in full bloom.

The only person who appeared not the least touched by this heartwarming atmosphere was Appleseed. He went about his declared business of counting the jug-money with great, persistent care. Every day now he came to the Valhalla and concentrated on the jug, scowling and mumbling to himself. At first we were all fascinated, but after a while, it got tiresome and nobody paid him any mind whatsoever. He never bought anything, apparently having never been able to raise the two bits. Sometimes he'd talk to Hamurabi, who had taken a tender interest in him and occasionally stood treat to a jawbreaker or a penny's worth of licorice.

'Do you still think he's nuts?' I asked.

'I'm not so sure,' said Hamurabi. 'But I'll let you know. He doesn't eat enough. I'm going to take him over to the Rainbow Café and buy him a plate of barbecue.'

'He'd appreciate it more if you'd give him a quarter.'

'No. A dish of barbecue is what he needs. Besides, it would be better if he never was to make a guess. A high-strung kid like that, so unusual, I wouldn't want to be the one responsible if he lost. Say, it would be pitiful.'

I'll admit that at the time Appleseed struck me as being just funny. Mr Marshall felt sorry for him, and the kids tried to tease him, but had to give it up when he refused to respond. There you could see him plain as day sitting at the fountain with his forehead puckered and his eyes fixed forever on that jug. Yet he was so withdrawn you sometimes had this awful creepy feeling that, well, maybe he didn't exist. And when you were pretty much convinced of this he'd wake up and say something like, 'You know, I hope a 1913 buffalo nickel's in there. A fella was tellin' me he saw where a 1913 buffalo nickel's worth fifty dollars.' Or, 'Middy's gonna be a big lady in the picture shows. They make lotsa money, the ladies in the picture shows do, and then we ain't gonna never eat another collard green as long as we live. Only Middy says she can't be in the picture shows 'less her teeth look good.'

Middy didn't always tag along with her brother. On those occasions when she didn't come, Appleseed wasn't himself; he acted shy and left soon.

Hamurabi kept his promise and stood treat to a dish of barbecue at the café. 'Mr Hamurabi's nice, all right,' said Appleseed afterwards, 'but he's got peculiar notions: has a notion that if he lived in this place named Egypt he'd be a king or somethin'.'

And Hamurabi said, 'That kid has the most touching faith. It's a beautiful thing to see. But I'm beginning to despise the whole business.' He gestured towards the jug. 'Hope of this kind is a cruel thing to give anybody, and I'm damned sorry I was ever a party to it.'

Around the Valhalla the most popular pastime was deciding what you would buy if you won the jug. Among those who participated were: Solomon Katz, Phoebe Jones, Carl Kuhnhardt, Puly Simmons, Addie Foxcroft, Marvin Finkle, Trudy Edwards and a coloured man named Erskine Washington. And these were some of their answers: a trip to and a permanent wave in Birmingham, a second-hand piano, a Shetland pony, a gold bracelet, a set of *Rover Boys* books and a life insurance policy.

Once Mr Marshall asked Appleseed what he would get. 'It's a secret,' was the reply, and no amount of prying could make him tell. We took it for granted that whatever it was, he wanted it real bad.

Honest winter, as a rule, doesn't settle on our part of the country till late January, and then is mild, lasting only a short time. But in the year of which I write we were blessed with a singular cold spell the week before Christmas. Some still talk of it, for it was so terrible: water pipes froze solid; many folks had to spend the days in bed snuggled under their quilts, having neglected to lay in enough kindling for the fireplace; the sky turned that strange dull grey as it does just before a storm, and the sun was pale as a waning moon. There was a sharp wind: the old dried-up leaves of last fall fell on the icy ground, and the evergreen tree in the courthouse square was twice stripped of its Christmas finery. When you breathed, your breath made smoky clouds. Down by the silk mill where the very poor people lived, the families huddled together in the dark at night and told tales to keep their minds off the cold. Out in the country the farmers covered their delicate plants with gunny sacks and prayed; some took advantage of the weather to slaughter their hogs and bring the fresh sausage to town. Mr R. C. Judkins, our town drunk, outfitted himself in a red cheesecloth suit and played Santa Claus at the five 'n' dime. Mr R. C. Judkins was the father of a big family, so everybody was happy to see him sober enough to earn a dollar. There were several church socials at one of which Mr Marshall came face to face with Rufus McPherson: bitter words were passed but not a blow was struck.

Now, as has been mentioned, Appleseed lived on a farm a mile below Indian Branches; this would be approximately three miles from town; a mighty long and lonesome walk. Still, despite the cold, he came every day to the Valhalla and stayed till closing time which, as the days had grown short, was after nightfall. Once in a while he'd catch a ride part way home with the foreman from the silk mill, but not often. He looked tired, and there were worry lines about his mouth. He was always cold and shivered a lot. I don't think he wore any warm drawers underneath his red sweater and blue britches.

It was three days before Christmas when out of the clear

sky, he announced: 'Well, I'm finished. I mean I know how much is in the bottle.' He claimed this with such grave, solemn sureness it was hard to doubt him.

'Why, say now, son, hold on,' said Hamurabi, who was present. 'You can't know anything of the sort. It's wrong to think so: you're just heading to get yourself hurt.'

'You don't need to preach to me, Mr Hamurabi. I know what I'm up to. A lady in Louisiana, she told me . . .'

'Yes yes yes – but you got to forget that. If it were me, I'd go home and stay put and forget about this god-dammed jug.'

'My brother's gonna play the fiddle at a wedding over in Cherokee City tonight and he's gonna give me the two bits,' said Appleseed stubbornly. 'Tomorrow I'll take my chance.'

So the next day I felt kind of excited when Appleseed and Middy arrived. Sure enough, he had his quarter: it was tied for safekeeping in the corner of a red bandanna.

The two of them wandered hand in hand among the show-cases, holding a whispery consultation as to what to purchase. They decided finally on a thimble-sized bottle of gardenia cologne which Middy promptly opened and partly emptied on her hair. 'I smells like . . . Oh, darlin' Mary, I ain't never smelled nothin' as sweet. Here, Appleseed, honey, let me douse some on your hair.' But he wouldn't let her.

Mr Marshall got out the ledger in which he kept his records, while Appleseed strolled over to the fountain and cupped the jug between his hands, stroking it gently. His eyes were bright and his cheeks flushed from excitement. Several persons who were in the drugstore at that moment crowded close. Middy stood in the background quietly scratching her leg and smelling the cologne. Hamurabi wasn't there.

Mr Marshall licked the point of his pencil and smiled. 'Okay, son, what do you say?'

Appleseed took a deep breath. 'Seventy-seven dollars and thirty-five cents,' he blurted.

In picking such an uneven sum he showed originality, for the run-of-the-mill guess was a plain round figure. Mr Marshall repeated the amount solemnly as he copied it down.

'When'll I know if I won?'

'Christmas Eve,' someone said.

'That's tomorrow, huh?'

'Why, so it is,' said Mr Marshall, not surprised. 'Come at four o'clock.'

During the night the thermometer dropped even lower, and towards dawn there was one of those swift, summerlike rainstorms, so that the following day was bright and frozen. The town was like a picture postcard of a Northern scene, what with icicles sparkling whitely on the trees and frost flowers coating all windowpanes. Mr R. C. Judkins rose early and, for no clear reason, tramped the streets ringing a supper bell, stopping now and then to take a swig of whisky from a pint which he kept in his hip pocket. As the day was windless, smoke climbed lazily from various chimneys straightway to the still, frozen sky. By mid-morning the Presbyterian choir was in full swing; and the town kids (wearing horror masks, as at Hallowe'en) were chasing one another round and round the square, kicking up an awful fuss.

Hamurabi dropped by at noon to help us fix up the Valhalla. He brought along a fat sack of Satsumas, and together we ate every last one, tossing the hulls into a newly installed potbellied stove (a present from Mr Marshall to himself) which stood in the middle of the room. Then my uncle took the jug off the fountain, polished and placed it on a prominently situated table. He was no help after that whatsoever, for he squatted in a chair and spent his time tying and retying a tacky green ribbon around the jug. So Hamurabi and I had the rest to do alone: we swept the floor and washed the mirrors and dusted the cabinets and strung streamers of red and green crepe paper from wall to wall. When we were finished it looked very fine and elegant.

But Hamurabi gazed sadly at our work, and said: 'Well, I think I better be getting along now.'

'Aren't you going to stay?' asked Mr Marshall, shocked.

'No, oh, no,' said Hamurabi, shaking his head slowly. 'I

don't want to see that kid's face. This is Christmas and I mean to have a rip-roaring time. And I couldn't, not with something like that on my conscience. Hell, I wouldn't sleep.'

'Suit yourself,' said Mr Marshall. And he shrugged, but you could see he was really hurt. 'Life's like that – and besides, who knows, he might win.'

Hamurabi sighed gloomily. 'What's his guess?'

'Seventy-seven dollars and thirty-five cents,' I said.

'Now I ask you, isn't that fantastic?' said Hamurabi. He slumped in a chair next to Mr Marshall and crossed his legs and lit a cigarette. 'If you got any Baby Ruths I think I'd like one; my mouth tastes sour.'

As the afternoon wore on, the three of us sat around the table feeling terribly blue. No one said hardly a word and, as the kids had deserted the square, the only sound was the clock tolling the hour in the courthouse steeple. The Valhalla was closed to business, but people kept passing by and peeking in the window. At three o'clock Mr Marshall told me to unlock the door.

Within twenty minutes the place was jam full; everyone was wearing his Sunday best, and the air smelled sweet, for most of the little silk-mill girls had scented themselves with vanilla flavouring. They crunched up against the walls, perched on the fountain, squeezed in wherever they could; soon the crowd had spread to the sidewalk and stretched into the road. The square was lined with team-drawn wagons and Model T Fords that had carted farmers and their families into town. There was much laughter and shouting and joking – several outraged ladies complained of the cursing and the rough, shoving ways of the younger men, but nobody left. At the side entrance a gang of coloured folks had formed and were having the most fun of all. Everybody was making the best of a good thing. It's usually so quiet around here: nothing much ever happens. It's safe to say that nearly all of Wachata County was present, but invalids and Rufus McPherson. I looked around for Appleseed but didn't see him anywhere.

Mr Marshall harumphed, and clapped for attention. When things quieted down and the atmosphere was properly tense, he raised his voice like an auctioneer, and called: 'Now, listen everybody, in this here envelope you see in my hand' – he held a manila envelope above his head – 'well, in it's the *answer* – which nobody but God and the First National Bank knows up to now, ha, ha. And in this book' – he held up the ledger with his free hand – 'I've got written down what you folks guessed. Are there any questions?' All was silence. 'Fine. Now, if we could have a volunteer . . .'

Not a living soul budged an inch: it was as if an awful shyness had overcome the crowd, and even those who were ordinarily natural-born show-offs shuffled their feet, ashamed. Then a voice, Appleseed's, hollered, 'Lemme by . . . Outa the way, please, ma'am.' Trotting along behind as he pushed forward were Middy and a lanky, sleepy-eyed fellow who was evidently the fiddling brother. Appleseed was dressed the same as usual, but his face was scrubbed rosy clean, his boots polished and his hair slicked back skin tight with Stacomb. 'Did we get here in time?' he panted.

But Mr Marshall said, 'So you want to be our volunteer?' Appleseed looked bewildered, then nodded vigorously.

'Does anybody have an objection to this young man?'

Still there was dead quiet. Mr Marshall handed the envelope to Appleseed who accepted it calmly. He chewed his under lip while studying it a moment before ripping the flap.

In all that congregation there was no sound except an occasional cough and the soft tinkling of Mr R. C. Judkins' supper bell. Hamurabi was leaning against the fountain, staring up at the ceiling; Middy was gazing blankly over her brother's shoulder, and when he started to tear open the envelope she let out a pained little gasp.

Appleseed withdrew a slip of pink paper and, holding it as though it was very fragile, muttered to himself whatever was written there. Suddenly his face paled and tears glistened in his eyes.

'Hey, speak up, boy,' someone hollered.

Hamurabi stepped forward and all but snatched the slip

away. He cleared his throat and commenced to read when his expression changed most comically. 'Well, Mother o' God...' he said.

'Louder! Louder!' an angry chorus demanded.

'Buncha crooks!' yelled Mr R. C. Judkins, who had a snootful by this time. 'I smelled a rat and he smells to high heaven!' Whereupon a cyclone of catcalls and whistling rent the air.

Appleseed's brother whirled round and shook his fist. 'Shudup, shuddup 'fore I bust every one of your goddamn heads together so's you got knots the size a musk melons, hear me?'

'Citizens,' cried Mayor Mawes, 'citizens – I say, this is Christmas ... I say ...'

And Mr Marshall hopped up on a chair and clapped and stamped till a minimum of order was restored. It might as well be noted here that we later found out Rufus McPherson had paid Mr R. C. Judkins to start the rumpus. Anyway, when the outbreak was quelled, who should be in possession of the slip but me ... don't ask how.

Without thinking, I shouted, 'Seventy-seven dollars and thirty-five cents.' Naturally, due to the excitement, I didn't at first catch the meaning; it was just a number. Then Appleseed's brother let forth with his whooping yell, and so I understood. The name of the winner spread quickly, and the awed, murmuring whispers were like a rainstorm.

Oh, Appleseed himself was a sorry sight. He was crying as though he was mortally wounded, but when Hamurabi lifted him onto his shoulders so the crowd could get a gander, he dried his eyes with the cuffs of his sweater and began grinning. Mr R. C. Judkins yelled, 'Gyp! Lousy gyp!' but was drowned out by a deafening round of applause.

Middy grabbed my arm. 'My teeth,' she squealed. 'Now I'm gonna get my teeth.'

'Teeth?' said I, kind of dazed.

'The false kind,' says she. 'That's what we're gonna get us with the money – a lovely set of white false teeth.'

But at that moment my sole interest was in how Appleseed had known. 'Hey, tell me,' I said desperately, 'tell me, how in

God's name did he know there was just exactly seventy-seven dollars and thirty-five cents?'

Middy gave me this *look*. 'Why, I thought he told you,' she said, real serious. 'He counted.'

'Yes, but how – how?'

'Gee, don't you even know how to count?'

'But is that all he did?'

'Well,' she said, following a thoughtful pause, 'he did do a little praying, too.' She started to dart off, then turned back and called, 'Besides, he was born with a caul on his head.'

And that's the nearest anybody ever came to solving the mystery. Thereafter, if you were to ask Appleseed 'How come?' he would smile strangely and change the subject. Many years later he and his family moved to somewhere in Florida and were never heard from again.

But in our town his legend flourishes still; and, till his death a year ago last April, Mr Marshall was invited each Christmas Day to tell the story of Appleseed to the Baptist Bible class. Hamurabi once typed up an account and mailed it around to various magazines. It was never printed. One editor wrote back and said that 'If the little girl really turned out to be a movie star, then there might be something to your story.' But that's not what happened, so why should you lie?

Miriam

For several years, Mrs H. T. Miller had lived alone in a pleasant apartment (two rooms with kitchenette) in a remodelled brownstone near the East River. She was a widow: Mr H. T. Miller had left a reasonable amount of insurance. Her interests were narrow, she had no friends to speak of, and she rarely journeyed farther than the corner grocery. The other people in the house never seemed to notice her: her clothes were matter-of-fact, her hair iron-grey, clipped and casually waved; she did not use cosmetics, her features were plain and inconspicuous, and on her last birthday she was sixty-one. Her activities were seldom spontaneous: she kept the two rooms immaculate, smoked an occasional cigarette, prepared her own meals and tended a canary.

Then she met Miriam. It was snowing that night. Mrs Miller had finished drying the supper dishes and was thumbing through an afternoon paper when she saw an advertisement of a picture playing at a neighbourhood theatre. The title sounded good, so she struggled into her beaver coat, laced her galoshes and left the apartment, leaving one light burning in the foyer: she found nothing more disturbing than a sensation of darkness.

The snow was fine, falling gently, not yet making an impression on the pavement. The wind from the river cut only at street crossings. Mrs Miller hurried, her head bowed, oblivious as a mole burrowing a blind path. She stopped at a drugstore and bought a package of peppermints.

A long line stretched in front of the box office; she took her place at the end. There would be (a tired voice groaned) a short wait for all seats. Mrs Miller rummaged in her leather handbag till she collected exactly the correct change for admission. The line seemed to be taking its own time and, looking around for some distraction, she suddenly became conscious of a little girl standing under the edge of the marquee.

Her hair was the longest and strangest Mrs Miller had ever seen: absolutely silver-white, like an albino's. It flowed waist-length in smooth, loose lines. She was thin and fragilely constructed. There was a simple, special elegance in the way she stood with her thumbs in the pockets of a tailored plum-velvet coat.

Mrs Miller felt oddly excited, and when the little girl glanced towards her, she smiled warmly. The little girl walked over and said, 'Would you care to do me a favour?'

'I'd be glad to, if I can,' said Mrs Miller.

'Oh, it's quite easy. I merely want you to buy a ticket for me; they won't let me in otherwise. Here, I have the money.' And gracefully she handed Mrs Miller two dimes and a nickel.

They went into the theatre together. An usherette directed them to a lounge; in twenty minutes the picture would be over.

'I feel just like a genuine criminal,' said Mrs Miller gaily, as she sat down. 'I mean that sort of thing's against the law, isn't it? I do hope I haven't done the wrong thing. Your mother knows where you are, dear? I mean she does, doesn't she?'

The little girl said nothing. She unbuttoned her coat and folded it across her lap. Her dress underneath was prim and dark blue. A gold chain dangled about her neck, and her fingers, sensitive and musical-looking, toyed with it. Examining her more attentively, Mrs Miller decided the truly distinctive feature was not her hair, but her eyes; they were hazel, steady, lacking any childlike quality whatsoever and, because of their size, seemed to consume her small face.

Mrs Miller offered a peppermint. 'What's your name, dear?'

'Miriam,' she said, as though, in some curious way, it were information already familiar.

'Why, isn't that funny – my name's Miriam, too. And it's not a terribly common name either. Now, don't tell me your last name's Miller!'

'Just Miriam.'

'But isn't that funny?'

'Moderately,' said Miriam, and rolled the peppermint on her tongue.

Mrs Miller flushed and shifted uncomfortably. 'You have such a large vocabulary for such a little girl.'

'Do I?'

'Well, yes,' said Mrs Miller, hastily changing the topic to: 'Do you like the movies?'

'I really wouldn't know,' said Miriam. 'I've never been before.'

Women began filling the lounge; the rumble of the newsreel bombs exploded in the distance. Mrs Miller rose, tucking her purse under her arm. 'I guess I'd better be running now if I want to get a seat,' she said. 'It was nice to have met you.'

Miriam nodded ever so slightly.

It snowed all week. Wheels and footsteps moved soundlessly on the street, as if the business of living continued secretly behind a pale but impenetrable curtain. In the falling quiet there was no sky or earth, only snow lifting in the wind, frosting the window glass, chilling the rooms, deadening and hushing the city. At all hours it was necessary to keep a lamp lighted and Mrs Miller lost track of the days: Friday was no different from Saturday and on Sunday she went to the grocery: closed, of course.

That evening she scrambled eggs and fixed a bowl of tomato soup. Then, after putting on a flannel robe and cold-creaming her face, she propped herself up in bed with a hotwater bottle under her feet. She was reading the *Times* when the doorbell rang. At first she thought it must be a mistake and whoever it was would go away. But it rang and rang and settled to a persistent buzz. She looked at the clock: a little after eleven; it did not seem possible, she was always asleep by ten.

Climbing out of bed, she trotted barefoot across the living room. 'I'm coming, please be patient.' The latch was caught; she turned it this way and that way and the bell never paused an instant. 'Stop it,' she cried. The bolt gave way and she opened the door an inch. 'What in heaven's name?'

'Hello,' said Miriam.

'Oh . . . why, hello,' said Mrs Miller, stepping hesitantly into the hall. 'You're that little girl.'

'I thought you'd never answer, but I kept my finger on the button; I knew you were home. Aren't you glad to see me?'

Mrs Miller did not know what to say. Miriam, she saw, wore the same plum-velvet coat and now she had also a beret to match; her white hair was braided in two shining plaits and looped at the ends with enormous white ribbons.

'Since I've waited so long, you could at least let me in,' she said.

'It's awfully late. . . .'

Miriam regarded her blankly. 'What difference does that make? Let me in. It's cold out here and I have on a silk dress.' Then, with a gentle gesture, she urged Mrs Miller aside and passed into the apartment.

She dropped her coat and beret on a chair. She was indeed wearing a silk dress. White silk. White silk in February. The skirt was beautifully pleated and the sleeves long; it made a faint rustle as she strolled about the room. 'I like your place,' she said. 'I like the rug, blue's my favourite colour.' She touched a paper rose in a vase on the coffee table. 'Imitation,' she commented wanly. 'How sad. Aren't imitations sad?' She seated herself on the sofa, daintily spreading her skirt.

'What do you want?' asked Mrs Miller.

'Sit down,' said Miriam. 'It makes me nervous to see people stand.'

Mrs Miller sank to a hassock. 'What do you want?' she repeated.

'You know, I don't think you're glad I came.'

For a second time Mrs Miller was without an answer; her hand motioned vaguely. Miriam giggled and pressed back on a mound of chintz pillows. Mrs Miller observed that the girl was less pale than she remembered; her cheeks were flushed.

'How did you know where I lived?'

Miriam frowned. 'That's no question at all. What's your name? What's mine?'

'But I'm not listed in the phone book.'

'Oh, let's talk about something else.'

Mrs Miller said, 'Your mother must be insane to let a child like you wander around at all hours of the night – and in such ridiculous clothes. She must be out of her mind.'

Miriam got up and moved to a corner where a covered bird cage hung from a ceiling chain. She peeked beneath the cover. 'It's a canary,' she said. 'Would you mind if I woke him? I'd like to hear him sing.'

'Leave Tommy alone,' said Mrs Miller, anxiously. 'Don't you dare wake him.'

'Certainly,' said Miriam. 'But I don't see why I can't hear him sing.' And then, 'Have you anything to eat? I'm starving! Even milk and a jam sandwich would be fine.'

'Look,' said Mrs Miller, rising from the hassock, 'look – if I make some nice sandwiches will you be a good child and run along home? It's past midnight, I'm sure.'

'It's snowing,' reproached Miriam. 'And cold and dark.'

'Well, you shouldn't have come here to begin with,' said Mrs Miller, struggling to control her voice. 'I can't help the weather. If you want anything to eat you'll have to promise to leave.'

Miriam brushed a braid against her cheek. Her eyes were thoughtful, as if weighing the proposition. She turned towards the bird cage. 'Very well,' she said, 'I promise.'

How old is she? Ten? Eleven? Mrs Miller, in the kitchen, unsealed a jar of strawberry preserves and cut four slices of bread. She poured a glass of milk and paused to light a cigarette. *And why has she come?* Her hand shook as she held the match, fascinated, till it burned her finger. The canary was singing; singing as he did in the morning and at no other time. 'Miriam,' she called, 'Miriam, I told you not to disturb Tommy.' There was no answer. She called again; all she heard was the canary. She inhaled the cigarette and discovered she had lighted the cork-tip end and – oh, really, she mustn't lose her temper.

She carried the food in on a tray and set it on the coffee table. She saw first that the bird cage still wore its night cover. And Tommy was singing. It gave her a queer sensation. And no one was in the room. Mrs Miller went through an alcove leading to her bedroom; at the door she caught her breath.

'What are you doing?' she asked.

Miriam glanced up and in her eyes there was a look that was not ordinary. She was standing by the bureau, a jewel case opened before her. For a minute she studied Mrs Miller, forcing their eyes to meet, and she smiled. 'There's nothing good here,' she said. 'But I like this.' Her hand held a cameo brooch. 'It's charming.'

'Suppose – perhaps you'd better put it back,' said Mrs Miller, feeling suddenly the need of some support. She leaned against the door frame; her head was unbearably heavy; a pressure weighted the rhythm of her heartbeat. The light seemed to flutter defectively. 'Please, child – a gift from my husband . . .'

'But it's beautiful and I want it,' said Miriam. '*Give it to me.*'

As she stood, striving to shape a sentence which would somehow save the brooch, it came to Mrs Miller there was no one to whom she might turn; she was alone; a fact that had not been among her thoughts for a long time. Its sheer emphasis was stunning. But here in her own room in the hushed snow-city were evidences she could not ignore or, she knew with startling clarity, resist.

Miriam ate ravenously, and when the sandwiches and milk were gone, her fingers made cobweb movements over the plate, gathering crumbs. The cameo gleamed on her blouse, the blonde profile like a trick reflection of its wearer. 'That was very nice,' she sighed, 'though now an almond cake or a cherry would be ideal. Sweets are lovely, don't you think?'

Mrs Miller was perched precariously on the hassock, smoking a cigarette. Her hair net had slipped lopsided and loose strands straggled down her face. Her eyes were stupidly concentrated on nothing and her cheeks were mottled in red patches, as though a fierce slap had left permanent marks.

'Is there a candy – a cake?'

Mrs Miller tapped ash on the rug. Her head swayed slightly

as she tried to focus her eyes. 'You promised to leave if I made the sandwiches,' she said.

'Dear me, did I?'

'It was a promise and I'm tired and I don't feel well at all.'

'Mustn't fret,' said Miriam. 'I'm only teasing.'

She picked up her coat, slung it over her arm, and arranged her beret in front of a mirror. Presently she bent close to Mrs Miller and whispered, 'Kiss me good night.'

'Please – I'd rather not,' said Mrs Miller.

Miriam lifted a shoulder, arched an eyebrow. 'As you like,' she said, and went directly to the coffee table, seized the vase containing the paper roses, carried it to where the hard surface of the floor lay bare, and hurled it downward. Glass sprayed in all directions and she stamped her foot on the bouquet.

Then slowly she walked to the door, but before closing it she looked back at Mrs Miller with a slyly innocent curiosity.

Mrs Miller spent the next day in bed, rising once to feed the canary and drink a cup of tea; she took her temperature and had none, yet her dreams were feverishly agitated; their un-balanced mood lingered even as she lay staring wide-eyed at the ceiling. One dream threaded through the others like an elusively mysterious theme in a complicated symphony, and the scenes it depicted were sharply outlined, as though sketched by a hand of gifted intensity : a small girl, wearing a bridal gown and a wreath of leaves, led a grey procession down a mountain path, and among them there was unusual silence till a woman at the rear asked, 'Where is she taking us?' 'No one knows,' said an old man marching in front. 'But isn't she pretty?' volunteered a third voice. 'Isn't she like a frost flower ... so shining and white?'

Tuesday morning she woke up feeling better; harsh slats of sunlight, slanting through Venetian blinds, shed a disrupting light on her unwholesome fancies. She opened the window to discover a thawed, mild-as-spring day; a sweep of clean new clouds crumpled against a vastly blue, out-of-season sky; and across the low line of roof-tops she could see the river and smoke curving from tug-boat stacks in a warm wind. A great silver truck ploughed the snow-banked street, its machine sound humming in the air.

After straightening the apartment, she went to the grocer's, cashed a cheque and continued to Schrafft's where she ate breakfast and chatted happily with the waitress. Oh, it was a wonderful day – more like a holiday – and it would be so foolish to go home.

She boarded a Lexington Avenue bus and rode up to Eighty-sixth Street; it was here that she had decided to do a little shopping.

She had no idea what she wanted or needed, but she idled along, intent only upon the passers-by, brisk and preoccupied, who gave her a disturbing sense of separateness.

It was while waiting at the corner of Third Avenue that she saw the man: an old man, bowlegged and stooped under an armload of bulging packages; he wore a shabby brown coat and a checkered cap. Suddenly she realized they were exchanging a smile: there was nothing friendly about this smile, it was merely two cold flickers of recognition. But she was certain she had never seen him before.

He was standing next to an El pillar, and as she crossed the street he turned and followed. He kept quite close; from the corner of her eye she watched his reflection wavering on the shop windows.

Then in the middle of the block she stopped and faced him. He stopped also and cocked his head, grinning. But what could she say? Do? Here, in broad daylight, on Eighty-sixth Street? It was useless and, despising her own helplessness, she quickened her steps.

Now Second Avenue is a dismal street, made from scraps and ends; part cobblestone, part asphalt, part cement; and its atmosphere of desertion is permanent. Mrs Miller walked five blocks without meeting anyone, and all the while the steady crunch of his footfalls in the snow stayed near. And when she came to a florist's shop, the sound was still with her. She hurried inside and watched through the glass door as the old man passed; he kept his eyes straight ahead and didn't slow his pace, but he did one strange, telling thing: he tipped his cap.

'Six white ones, did you say?' asked the florist. 'Yes,' she told him, 'white roses'. From there she went to a glassware store and selected a vase, presumably a replacement for the one Miriam had broken, though the price was intolerable and the vase itself (she thought) grotesquely vulgar. But a series of unaccountable purchases had begun, as if by prearranged plan: a plan of which she had not the least knowledge or control.

She bought a bag of glazed cherries, and at a place called the Knickerbocker Bakery she paid forty cents for six almond cakes.

Within the last hour the weather had turned cold again; like blurred lenses, winter clouds cast a shade over the sun, and the skeleton of an early dusk coloured the sky; a damp mist mixed with the wind and the voices of a few children who romped high on mountains of gutter snow seemed lonely and cheerless. Soon the first flake fell, and when Mrs Miller reached the brownstone house, snow was falling in a swift screen and foot tracks vanished as they were printed.

The white roses were arranged decoratively in the vase. The glazed cherries shone on a ceramic plate. The almond cakes, dusted with sugar, awaited a hand. The canary fluttered on its swing and picked at a bar of seed.

At precisely five the doorbell rang. Mrs Miller *knew* who it was. The hem of her housecoat trailed as she crossed the floor. 'Is that you?' she called.

'Naturally,' said Miriam, the word resounding shrilly from the hall. 'Open this door.'

'Go away,' said Mrs Miller.

'Please hurry . . . I have a heavy package.'

'Go away,' said Mrs Miller. She returned to the living room, lighted a cigarette, sat down and calmly listened to the buzzer; on and on and on. 'You might as well leave. I have no intention of letting you in.'

Shortly the bell stopped. For possibly ten minutes Mrs Miller did not move. Then, hearing no sound, she concluded Miriam had gone. She tiptoed to the door and opened it a sliver; Miriam was half-reclining atop a cardboard box with a beautiful French doll cradled in her arms.

'Really, I thought you were never coming,' she said peevishly. 'Here, help me get this in, it's awfully heavy.'

It was not spell-like compulsion that Mrs Miller felt, but rather a curious passivity; she brought in the box, Miriam the doll. Miriam curled up on the sofa, not troubling to remove her coat or beret, and watched disinterestedly as Mrs Miller dropped the box and stood trembling, trying to catch her breath.

'Thank you,' she said. In the daylight she looked pinched and drawn, her hair less luminous. The French doll she was loving wore an exquisite powdered wig and its idiot glass eyes sought solace in Miriam's. 'I have a surprise,' she continued. 'Look into my box.'

Kneeling, Mrs Miller parted the flaps and lifted out another doll; then a blue dress which she recalled as the one Miriam had worn that first night at the theatre; and of the remainder she said, 'It's all clothes. Why?'

'Because I've come to live with you,' said Miriam, twisting a cherry stem. 'Wasn't it nice of you to buy me the cherries...?'

'But you can't! For God's sake go away – go away and leave me alone!'

'... and the roses and the almond cakes? How really wonderfully generous. You know, these cherries are delicious. The last place I lived was with an old man; he was terribly poor and we never had good things to eat. But I think I'll be happy here.' She paused to snuggle her doll closer. 'Now, if you'll just show me where to put my things...'

Mrs Miller's face dissolved into a mask of ugly red lines; she began to cry, and it was an unnatural, tearless sort of weeping, as though, not having wept for a long time, she had forgotten how. Carefully she edged backward till she touched the door.

She fumbled through the hall and down the stairs to a landing below. She pounded frantically on the door of the first apartment she came to; a short, red-headed man answered and she pushed past him. 'Say, what the hell is this?' he said.

'Anything wrong, lover?' asked a young woman who appeared from the kitchen, drying her hands. And it was to her that Mrs Miller turned.

'Listen,' she cried, 'I'm ashamed behaving this way but – well, I'm Mrs H. T. Miller and I live upstairs and ...' She pressed her hands over her face. 'It sounds so absurd. ...'

The woman guided her to a chair, while the man excitedly rattled pocket change. 'Yeah?'

'I live upstairs and there's a little girl visiting me, and I suppose that I'm afraid of her. She won't leave and I can't make her and – she's going to do something terrible. She's already stolen my cameo, but she's about to do something worse – something terrible!'

The man asked, 'Is she a relative, huh?'

Mrs Miller shook her head. 'I don't know who she is. Her name's Miriam, but I don't know for certain who she is.'

'You gotta calm down, honey,' said the woman, stroking Mrs Miller's arm. 'Harry here'll tend to this kid. Go on, lover.' And Mrs Miller said, 'The door's open – 5A.'

After the man left, the woman brought a towel and bathed Mrs Miller's face. 'You're very kind,' Mrs Miller said. 'I'm sorry to act like such a fool, only this wicked child ...'

'Sure, honey,' consoled the woman. 'Now, you better take it easy.'

Mrs Miller rested her head in the crook of her arm; she was quiet enough to be asleep. The woman turned a radio dial; a piano and a husky voice filled the silence and the woman, tapping her foot, kept excellent time. 'Maybe we oughta go up too,' she said.

'I don't want to see her again. I don't want to be anywhere near her.'

'Uh huh, but what you shoulda done, you shoulda called a cop.'

Presently they heard the man on the stairs. He strode into the room frowning and scratching the back of his neck. 'Nobody there,' he said, honestly embarrassed. 'She musta beat it.'

'Harry, you're a jerk,' announced the woman. 'We been

sitting here the whole time and we woulda seen . . .' she stopped abruptly, for the man's glance was sharp.

'I looked all over,' he said, 'and there just ain't nobody there. Nobody, understand?'

'Tell me,' said Mrs Miller, rising, 'tell me, did you see a large box? Or a doll?'

'No, ma'am, I didn't.'

And the woman, as if delivering a verdict, said, 'Well, for cryin' out loud. . . .'

Mrs Miller entered her apartment softly; she walked to the centre of the room and stood quite still. No, in a sense it had not changed: the roses, the cakes, and the cherries were in place. But this was an empty room, emptier than if the furnishings and familiars were not present, lifeless and petrified as a funeral parlour. The sofa loomed before her with a new strangeness: its vacancy had a meaning that would have been less penetrating and terrible had Miriam been curled on it. She gazed fixedly at the space where she remembered setting the box and, for a moment, the hassock spun desperately. And she looked through the window; surely the river was real, surely snow was falling – but then, one could not be certain witness to anything: Miriam, so vividly *there* – and yet, where was she? Where, where?

As though moving in a dream, she sank to a chair. The room was losing shape; it was dark and getting darker and there was nothing to be done about it; she could not lift her hand to light a lamp.

Suddenly, closing her eyes, she felt an upward surge, like a diver emerging from some deeper, greener depth. In times of terror or immense distress, there are moments when the mind waits, as though for a revelation, while a skein of calm is woven over thought; it is like a sleep, or a supernatural trance; and during this lull one is aware of a force of quiet reasoning: well, what if she had never really known a girl named Miriam? that she had been foolishly frightened on the street? In the end, like everything else, it was of no importance. For the only thing she had lost to Miriam was her identity, but now she knew she had found again the person who lived in this room, who cooked her own meals, who owned a canary, who was someone she could trust and believe in: Mrs H. T. Miller.

Listening in contentment, she became aware of a double sound: a bureau drawer opening and closing; she seemed to hear it long after completion – opening and closing. Then gradually, the harshness of it was replaced by the murmur of a silk dress and this, delicately faint, was moving nearer and swelling in intensity till the walls trembled with the vibration and the room was caving under a wave of whispers. Mrs Miller stiffened and opened her eyes to a dull, direct stare.

'Hello,' said Miriam.

The Headless Hawk

> They are of those that rebel against the light; they know not the ways thereof, nor abide in the paths thereof. In the dark they dig through houses, which they had marked for themselves in the daytime: they know not the light. For the morning is to them as the shadow of death: if one know them, they are in the terrors of the shadow of death.
>
> JOB 24: 13, 16, 17

Vincent switched off the lights in the gallery. Outside, after locking the door, he smoothed the brim of an elegant Panama, and started towards Third Avenue, his umbrella-cane tap-tap-tapping along the pavement. A promise of rain had darkened the day since dawn, and a sky of bloated clouds blurred the five o'clock sun; it was hot, though, humid as tropical mist, and voices, sounding along the grey July street, sounding muffled and strange, carried a fretful undertone. Vincent felt as though he moved below the sea. Buses, cruising crosstown through Fifty-seventh Street, seemed like green-bellied fish, and faces loomed and rocked like wave-riding masks. He studied each passer-by, hunting one, and presently he saw her, a girl in a green raincoat. She was standing on the downtown corner of Fifty-seventh and Third, just standing there smoking a cigarette, and giving somehow the impression she hummed a tune. The raincoat was transparent. She wore dark slacks, no socks, a pair of huaraches, a man's white shirt. Her hair was fawn-coloured, and cut like a boy's. When she noticed Vincent crossing towards her, she dropped the cigarette and hurried down the block to the doorway of an antique store.

Vincent slowed his step. He pulled out a handkerchief and dabbed his forehead; if only he could get away, go up to the Cape, lie in the sun. He bought an afternoon paper, and fumbled his change. It rolled in the gutter, dropped silently out of sight down a sewer grating. 'Ain't but a nickel, bub,' said the newsdealer, for Vincent, though actually unaware of his loss, looked heartbroken. And it was like that often now, never quite in contact, never sure whether a step would take him backward or forward, up or down. Very casually, with the handle of the umbrella hooked over an arm, and his eyes concentrated on the paper's headlines – but what did the damn thing say? – he continued downtown. A swarthy woman carrying a shopping bag jostled him, glared, muttered in coarsely vehement Italian. The ragged cut of her voice seemed to come through layers of wool. As he approached the antique store where the girl in the green raincoat waited, he walked slower still, counting one, two, three, four, five, six – at six he halted before the window.

The window was like a corner of an attic; a lifetime's discardings rose in a pyramid of no particular worth: vacant picture frames, a lavender wig, Gothic shaving mugs, beaded lamps. There was an oriental mask suspended on a ceiling cord, and wind from an electric fan whirling inside the shop revolved it slowly round and round. Vincent, by degrees, lifted his gaze, and looked at the girl directly. She was hovering in the doorway so that he saw her greenness distorted wavy through double glass; the elevated pounded overhead and the window trembled. Her image spread like a reflection on silverware, then gradually hardened again: she was watching him.

He hung an Old Gold between his lips, rummaged for a match and, finding none, sighed. The girl stepped from the doorway. She held out a cheap little lighter; as the flame pulsed up, her eyes, pale, shallow, cat-green, fixed him with alarming intensity. Her eyes had an astonished, a shocked look, as though, having at one time witnessed a terrible incident, they'd locked wide open. Carefree bangs fringed her forehead; this boy haircut emphasized the childish and rather poetic quality of her narrow, hollow-cheeked face. It was the kind of face one sometimes sees in paintings of medieval youths.

Letting the smoke pour out of his nose, Vincent, knowing it was useless to ask, wondered, as always, what she was living on, and where. He flipped away the cigarette, for he had not wanted it to begin with, and then, pivoting, crossed rapidly under the El; as he approached the kerb he heard a crash of brakes, and suddenly, as if cotton plugs had been blasted from his ears, city noises crowded in. A cab driver hollered: 'Fa crissake, sistuh, get the lead outa yuh pants!' but the girl did not even bother turning her head; trance-eyed, undisturbed as a sleepwalker, and staring straight at Vincent, who watched dumbly, she moved across the street. A coloured boy wearing a jazzy purple suit took her elbow. 'You sick, Miss?' he said, guiding her forward, and she did not answer. 'You look mighty funny, Miss. If you sick, I . . .' then, following the direction of her eyes, he released his hold. There was something here which made him all still inside. 'Uh – yeah,' he muttered, backing off with a grinning display of tartar-coated teeth.

So Vincent began walking in earnest, and his umbrella tapped code-like block after block. His shirt was soaked through with itchy sweat, and the noises, now so harsh, banged in his head: a trick car horn hooting 'My Country, 'Tis of Thee,' electric spray of sparks crackling bluely off thundering rails, whisky laughter hiccuping through gaunt doors of beer-stale bars where orchid juke machines manufactured U.S.A. music – 'I got spurs that jingle jangle jingle. . . .' Occasionally he caught a glimpse of her, once mirrored in the window of Paul's Seafood Palace where scarlet lobsters basked on a beach of flaked ice. She followed close with her hands shoved into the pockets of her raincoat. The brassy lights of a movie marquee blinked, and he remembered how she loved movies: murder films, spy chillers, Wild West shows. He turned into a side street leading towards the East River; it was quiet here, hushed like Sunday: a sailor-stroller munching an Eskimo pie, energetic twins skipping rope, an old velvety lady with gardenia-white hair lifting aside lace curtains and peering listlessly into rain-dark space – a city landscape in July. And behind him the soft insistent slap of sandals. Traffic lights on Second Avenue turned red; at the corner a bearded midget, Ruby the Popcorn Man, wailed, 'Hot buttered popcorn, big bag, yah?' Vincent shook his head, and the midget looked very put out, then: 'Yuh see?' he jeered, pushing a shovel inside of the candlelit cage where bursting kernels bounced like crazy moths. 'Yuh see, de girlie knows popcorn's nourishin'.' She bought a dime's worth, and it was in a green sack matching her raincoat, matching her eyes.

This is my neighbourhood, my street, the house with the gateway is where I live. To remind himself of this was necessary, inasmuch as he'd substituted for a sense of reality a knowledge of time, and place. He glanced gratefully at sourfaced, faded ladies, at the pipe-puffing males squatting on the surrounding steps of brownstone stoops. Nine pale little girls shrieked round a corner flower cart begging daisies to pin in their hair, but the peddler said, 'Shoo!' and, fleeing like beads of a broken bracelet, they circled in the street, the wild ones leaping with laughter, and the shy ones, silent and isolated, lifting summer-wilted faces skyward : the rain, would it never come?

Vincent, who lived in a basement apartment, descended several steps and took out his keycase; then, pausing behind the hallway door, he looked back through a peephole in the panelling. The girl was waiting on the sidewalk above: she leaned against a brownstone banister, and her arms fell limp – and popcorn spilled snowlike round her feet. A grimy little boy crept slyly up to pick among it like a squirrel.

2

For Vincent it was a holiday. No one had come by the gallery all morning, which, considering the arctic weather, was not unusual. He sat at his desk devouring tangerines, and enjoying immensely a Thurber story in an old *New Yorker*. Laughing loudly, he did not hear the girl enter, see her cross the dark carpet, notice her at all, in fact, until the telephone rang. 'Garland Gallery, hello.' She was odd, most certainly, that indecent haircut, those depthless eyes – 'Oh, Paul. *Comme ci, comme ca*, and you?' – and dressed like a freak : no coat, just a lumberjack's shirt, navy-blue slacks and – was it a joke? – pink ankle socks, a pair of huaraches. 'The ballet? Who's dancing? Oh, her!' Under an arm she carried a flat parcel wrapped in sheets of funny-paper – 'Look, Paul, what say I call back?

There's someone here . . .' and, anchoring the receiver, assuming a commercial smile, he stood up. 'Yes?'

Her lips, crusty with chap, trembled with unrealized words as though she had possibly a defect of speech, and her eyes rolled in their sockets like loose marbles. It was the kind of disturbed shyness one associates with children. 'I've a picture,' she said. 'You buy pictures?'

At this, Vincent's smile became fixed. 'We exhibit.'

'I painted it myself,' she said, and her voice, hoarse and slurred, was Southern. 'My picture – I painted it. A lady told me there were places around here that bought pictures.'

Vincent said, 'Yes, of course, but the truth is' – and he made a helpless gesture – 'the truth is I've no authority whatever. Mr Garland – this is his gallery, you know – is out of town.' Standing there on the expanse of fine carpet, her body sagging sideways with the weight of her package, she looked like a sad rag doll. 'Maybe,' he began, 'maybe Henry Krueger up the street at Sixty-five . . .' but she was not listening.

'I did it myself,' she insisted softly. 'Tuesdays and Thursdays were our painting days, and a whole year I worked. The others, they kept messing it up, and Mr Destronelli . . .' Suddenly, as though aware of an indiscretion, she stopped and bit her lip. Her eyes narrowed. 'He's not a friend of yours?'

'Who?' said Vincent, confused.

'Mr Destronelli.'

He shook his head, and wondered why it was that eccentricity always excited in him such curious admiration. It was the feeling he'd had as a child toward carnival freaks. And it was true that about those whom he'd loved there was always a little something wrong, broken. Strange, though, that this quality, having stimulated an attraction, should, in his case, regularly end it by destroying it. 'Of course I haven't any authority,' he repeated, sweeping tangerine hulls into a wastebasket, 'but, if you like, I suppose I could look at your work.'

A pause; then, kneeling on the floor, she commenced stripping off the funny-paper wrapping. It originally had been, Vincent noticed, part of the New Orleans *Times-Picayune*. 'From the South, aren't you?' he said. She did not look up, but he saw her shoulders stiffen. 'No,' she said. Smiling, he considered a moment, decided it would be tactless to challenge so transparent a lie. Or could she have misunderstood? And all at once he felt an intense longing to touch her head, finger her boyish hair. He shoved his hands in his pockets and glanced at the window. It was spangled with February frost, and some passerby had scratched on the glass an obscenity.

'There,' she said.

A headless figure in a monklike robe reclined complacently on top a tacky vaudeville trunk; in one hand she held a fuming blue candle, in the other a miniature gold cage, and her severed head lay bleeding at her feet: it was the girl's, this head, but here her hair was long, very long, and a snowball kitten with crystal spitfire eyes playfully pawed, as it would a spool of yarn, the sprawling ends. The wings of a hawk, headless, scarlet-breasted, copper-clawed, curtained the background like a nightfall sky. It was a crude painting, the hard pure colours moulded with male brutality, and, while there was not technical merit evident, it had that power often seen in something deeply felt, though primitively conveyed. Vincent reacted as he did when occasionally a phrase of music surprised a note of inward recognition, or a cluster of words in a poem revealed to him a secret concerning himself: he felt a powerful chill of pleasure run down his spine. 'Mr Garland is in Florida,' he said cautiously, 'but I think he should see it; you couldn't leave it for, say, a week?'

'I had a ring and I sold it,' she said, and he had the feeling she was talking in a trance. 'It was a nice ring, a wedding ring – not mine – with writing on it. I had an overcoat, too.' She twisted one of her shirt buttons, pulled till it popped off and rolled on the carpet like a pearl eye. 'I don't want much – fifty dollars; is that unfair?'

'Too much,' said Vincent, more curtly than he intended. Now he wanted her painting, not for the gallery, but for himself. There are certain works of art which excite more interest in their creators than in what they have created, usually because in this kind of work one is able to identify something which has until that instant seemed a private inexpressible perception, and you wonder: who is this that knows me, and how? 'I'll give thirty.'

For a moment she gaped at him stupidly, and then, sucking her breath, held out her hand, palm up. This directness, too innocent to be offensive, caught him off guard. Somewhat embarrassed, he said, 'I'm most awfully afraid I'll have to mail a cheque. Could you . . . ?' The telephone interrupted, and, as he went to answer, she followed, her hand outstretched, a frantic look pinching her face. 'Oh, Paul, may I call back? Oh, I see. Well, hold on a sec.' Cupping the mouthpiece against his shoulder, he pushed a pad and pencil across the desk. 'Here, write your name and address.'

But she shook her head, the dazed, anxious expression deepening.

'*Cheque*,' said Vincent, 'I have to mail a cheque. Please, your name and address.' He grinned encouragingly when at last she began to write.

'Sorry, Paul . . . Whose party? Why, the little bitch, she didn't invite . . . Hey!' he called, for the girl was moving towards the door. 'Please, hey!' Cold air chilled the gallery, and the door slammed with a glassy rattle. Hellohellohello. Vincent did not answer; he stood puzzling over the curious information she'd left printed on his pad: D. J. – Y.W.C.A. Hellohellohello.

It hung above his mantel, the painting, and on those nights when he could not sleep he would pour a glass of whisky and talk to the headless hawk, tell it the stuff of his life: he was, he said, a poet who had never written poetry, a painter who had never painted, a lover who had never loved (absolutely) – someone, in short, without direction, and quite headless. Oh, it wasn't that he hadn't tried – good beginnings, always, bad endings, always. Vincent, white, male, age 36, college graduate: a man in the sea, fifty miles from shore; a victim, born to be murdered, either by himself or another; an actor unemployed. It was there, all of it, in the painting, everything disconnected and cockeyed, and who was she that she should know so much? Inquiries, those he'd made, had led nowhere, not another dealer knew of her, and to search for a D. J. living in, presumably, a Y.W.C.A. seemed absurd. Then, too, he'd quite expected she would reappear, but February passed, and March. One evening, crossing the square which fronts the Plaza, he had a queer thing happen. The archaic hansom drivers who line that location were lighting their carriage lamps, for it was dusk, and lamplight traced through moving leaves. A hansom pulled from the curb and rolled past in the twilight. There was a single occupant, and this passenger, whose face he could not see, was a girl with chopped fawn-coloured hair. So he settled on a bench, and whiled away time talking with a soldier, and a fairy coloured boy who quoted poetry, and a man out airing a dachshund : night characters with whom he waited – but the carriage, with the one for whom he waited, never came back. Again he saw her (or supposed he did) descending subway stairs, and this time lost her in the tiled tunnels of painted arrows and Spearmint machines. It was as if her face were imposed upon his mind; he could no more dispossess it than could, for example, a dead man rid his legendary eyes of the last image seen. Around the middle of April he went up to Connecticut to spend a week-end with his married sister : keyed-up, caustic, he wasn't, as she complained, at all like himself. 'What is it, Vinny, darling – if you need money . . . ' 'Oh, shut up!' he said. 'Must be love,' teased his brother-in-law. 'Come on, Vinny, 'fess up; what's she like?' And all this so annoyed him he caught the next train home. From a booth in Grand Central he called to apologize, but a sick nervousness hummed inside him, and he hung up while the operator was still trying to make a connexion. He wanted a drink. At the Commodore Bar he spent an hour or so drowning four daiquiris – it was Saturday, it was nine, there was nothing to do unless he did it alone, he was feeling sad for himself. Now in the park behind the Public Library sweethearts moved whisperingly under trees, and drinking-fountain water bubbled softly, like their voices, but for all the white April evening meant to him, Vincent, drunk a little and wandering, might as well have been old, like the old bench-sitters rasping phlegm.

In the country, spring is a time of small happenings happening quietly, hyacinth shoots thrusting in a garden, willows burning with a sudden frosty fire of green, lengthening afternoons of long flowing dusk, and midnight rain opening lilac; but in the city there is the fanfare of organ-grinders, and odours, undiluted by winter wind, clog the air; windows long closed go up, and conversation, drifting beyond a room, collides with the jangle of a peddler's bell. It is the crazy season of toy balloons and roller skates, of courtyard baritones and men of freakish enterprise, like the one who jumped up now like a jack-in-the-box. He was old, he had a telescope and a sign: 25c See the Moon! See the Stars! 25c! No stars could penetrate a city's glare, but Vincent saw the moon, a round, shadowed whiteness, and then a blaze of electric bulbs: Four Roses, Bing Cro— he was moving through caramel-scented staleness, swimming through oceans of cheese-pale faces, neon, and darkness. Above the blasting of a jukebox, bulletfire boomed, a cardboard duck fell plop, and somebody screeched: 'Yay Iggy!' It was a Broadway funhouse, a penny arcade, and jammed from wall to wall with Saturday splurgers. He watched a penny movie (*What the Bootblack Saw*), and had his fortune told by a wax witch leering behind glass: 'Yours is an affectionate nature' . . . but he read no further, for up near the jukebox there was an attractive commotion. A crowd of kids, clapping in time to jazz music, had formed a circle around two dancers. These dancers were both coloured, both girls. They swayed together slow and easy, like lovers, rocked and stamped and rolled serious savage eyes, their muscles rhythmically attuned to the ripple of a clarinet, the rising harangue of a drum. Vincent's gaze travelled round the audience, and when he saw her a bright shiver went through him, for something of the dance's violence was reflected in her face. Standing there beside a tall ugly boy, it was as if she were the sleeper and the Negroes a dream. Trumpet-drum-piano, bawling on behind a black girl's froggy voice, wailed towards a rocking finale. The clapping ended, the dancers parted. She was alone now; though Vincent's instinct was to leave before she noticed, he advanced, and, as one would gently waken a sleeper, lightly touched her shoulder. 'Hello,' he said, his voice too loud.

Turning, she stared at him, and her eyes were clear-blank. First terror, then puzzlement replaced the dead lost look. She took a step backward, and, just as the jukebox commenced hollering again, he seized her wrist: 'You remember me,' he prompted, 'the gallery? Your painting?' She blinked, let the lids sink sleepily over those eyes, and he could feel the slow relaxing of tension in her arm. She was thinner than he recalled, prettier, too, and her hair, grown out somewhat, hung in casual disorder. A little silver Christmas ribbon dangled sadly from a stray lock. He started to say, 'Can I buy you a drink?' but she leaned against him, her head resting on his chest like a child's, and he said: 'Will you come home with me?' She lifted her face; the answer, when it came, was a breath, a whisper: 'Please,' she said.

Vincent stripped off his clothes, arranged them neatly in the closet, and admired his nakedness before a mirrored door. He was not so handsome as he supposed, but handsome all the same. For his moderate height he was excellently proportioned; his hair was dark yellow, and his delicate, rather snub-nosed face had a fine, ruddy colouring. The rumble of running water broke the quiet; she was in the bathroom preparing to bathe. He dressed in loose-fitting flannel pyjamas, lit a cigarette, said, 'Everything all right?' The water went off, a long silence, then: 'Yes, thank you.' On the way home in a cab he'd made an attempt at conversation, but she had said nothing, not even when they entered the apartment – and this last offended him, for, taking rather female pride in his quarters, he'd expected a complimentary remark. It was one enormously high-ceilinged room, a bath and kitchenette, a backyard garden. In the furnishings he'd combined modern with antique and produced a distinguished result. Decorating the walls were a trio of Toulouse-Lautrec prints, a framed circus poster, D. J.'s painting, photographs of Rilke, Nijinsky and Duse. A candelabra of lean blue candles burned on a desk; the room, washed in their delirious light, wavered. French doors led into the yard. He never used it much, for it was a place impossible to keep clean. There were a few dead tulip stalks dark in the moonshine, a puny heaven tree, and an old weather-worn chair left by the last tenant. He paced back and forth over the cold flagstones, hoping that in the cool air the drugged drunk sensation he felt would wear off. Nearby a piano was being badly mauled, and in a window above there was a child's face. He was thumbing a blade of grass when her shadow fell long across the yard. She was in the doorway. 'You mustn't come out,' he said, moving towards her. 'It's turned a little cold.'

There was about her now an appealing softness; she seemed somehow less angular, less out of tune with the average, and Vincent, offering a glass of sherry, was delighted at the delicacy with which she touched it to her lips. She was wearing his terry-cloth robe; it was by yards too large. Her feet were bare, and she tucked them up beside her on the couch. 'It's like Glass Hill, the candlelight,' she said, and smiled. 'My Granny lived at Glass Hill. We had lovely times, sometimes; do you know what she used to say? She used to say, "Candles are magic wands; light one and the world is a story book".'

'What a dreary old lady she must've been,' said Vincent, quite drunk. 'We should probably have hated each other.'

'Granny would've loved you,' she said. 'She loved any kind of man, every man she ever met, even Mr Destronelli.'

'Destronelli?' It was a name he'd heard before.

Her eyes slid slyly sideways, and this look seemed to say: There must be no subterfuge between us, we who understand each other have no need of it. 'Oh, you know,' she said with a conviction that, under more commonplace circumstances would have been surprising. It was, however, as if he'd abandoned temporarily the faculty of surprise. 'Everybody knows him.'

He curved an arm around her, and brought her nearer. 'Not me, I don't,' he said, kissing her mouth, neck; she was not responsive especially, but he said – and his voice had gone adolescently shaky – 'Never met Mr Whoozits.' He slipped a hand inside her robe, loosening it away from her shoulders. Above one breast she had a birthmark, small and star-shaped. He glanced at the mirrored door where uncertain light rippled their reflections, made them pale and incomplete. She was smiling. 'Mr Whoozits,' he said, 'what does he look like?' The suggestion of a smile faded, a small monkeylike frown flickered on her face. She looked above the mantel at her painting, and he realized that this was the first notice she'd shown it; she appeared to study in the picture a particular object, but whether hawk or head he could not say. 'Well,' she said quietly, pressing closer to him, 'he looks like you, like me, like most anybody.'

It was raining; in the wet noon light two nubs of candle still burned, and at an open window grey curtains tossed forlornly. Vincent extricated his arm; it was numb from the weight of her body. Careful not to make a noise, he eased out of bed, blew out the candles, tiptoed into the bathroom and doused his face with cold water. On the way to the kitchenette he flexed his arms, feeling, as he hadn't for a long time, an intensely male pleasure in his strength, a healthy wholeness of person. He made and put on a tray orange juice, raisin-bread toast, a pot of tea; then, so inexpertly that everything on the tray rattled, he brought the breakfast in and placed it on a table beside the bed.

She had not moved; her ruffled hair spread fanwise across the pillow, and one hand rested in the hollow where his head had lain. He leaned over and kissed her lips, and her eyelids, blue with sleep, trembled. 'Yes, yes, I'm awake,' she murmured, and rain, lifting in the wind, sprayed against the window like surf. He somehow knew that with her there would be none of the usual artifice, no avoidance of eyes, no shamefaced, accusing pause. She raised herself on her elbow; she looked at him, Vincent thought, as if he were her husband, and, handing her the orange juice, he smiled his gratitude.

'What is today?'

'Sunday,' he told her, bundling under the quilt, and settling the tray across his legs.

'But there are no church bells,' she said. 'And it's raining.'

Vincent divided a piece of toast. 'You don't mind that, do you? Rain – such a peaceful sound.' He poured tea. 'Sugar? Cream?'

She disregarded this, and said, 'Today is Sunday what? What month, I mean?'

'Where have you been living, in the subway?' he said, grinning. And it puzzled him to think she was serious. 'Oh, April ... April something-or-other.'

'April,' she repeated. 'Have I been here long?'

'Only since last night.'

'Oh.'

Vincent stirred his tea, the spoon tinkling in the cup like a bell. Toast crumbs spilled among the sheets, and he thought of the *Tribune* and the *Times* waiting outside the door, but they, this morning, held no charms; it was best lying here beside her in the warm bed, sipping tea, listening to the rain. Odd, when you stopped to consider, certainly very odd. She did not know his name, nor he hers. And so he said, 'I still owe you thirty dollars, do you realize that? Your own fault, of course – leaving such a damn fool address. And D.J., what is that supposed to mean?'

'I don't think I'd better tell you my name,' she said. 'I could make up one easy enough: Dorothy Jordan, Delilah Johnson; see? There are all kinds of names I could make up, and if it wasn't for him I'd tell you right.'

Vincent lowered the tray to the floor. He rolled over on his side, and, facing her, his heartbeat quickened. 'Who's him?' Though her expression was calm, anger muddied her voice when she said, 'If you don't know him, then tell me, why am I here?'

Silence, and outside the rain seemed suddenly suspended. A ship's horn moaned in the river. Holding her close, he combed his fingers through her hair, and, wanting so much to be believed, said, 'Because I love you.'

She closed her eyes. 'What became of them?'

'Who?'

'The others you've said that to.'

It commenced again, the rain spattering greyly at the window, falling on hushed Sunday streets; listening, Vincent remembered. He remembered his cousin, Lucille, poor, beautiful, stupid Lucille who sat all day embroidering silk flowers on scraps of linen. And Allen T. Baker – there was the winter they'd spent in Havana, the house they'd lived in, crumbling rooms of rose-coloured rock; poor Allen, he'd thought it was to be forever. Gordon, too. Gordon, with the kinky yellow hair, and a head full of old Elizabethan ballads. Was it true he'd shot himself? And Connie Silver, the deaf girl, the one who had wanted to be an actress – what had become of her? Or Helen, Louise, Laura? 'There was just one,' he said, and to his own ears, this had a truthful ring. 'Only one, and she's dead.'

Tenderly, as if in sympathy, she touched his cheek. 'I suppose he killed her,' she said, her eyes so close he could see the outline of his face imprisoned in their greenness. 'He killed Miss Hall, you know. The dearest woman in the world, Miss Hall, and so pretty your breath went away. I had piano lessons with her, and when she played the piano, when she said hello and when she said good-bye – it was like my heart would stop.' Her voice had taken on an impersonal tone, as though she were talking of matters belonging to another age, and in which she was not concerned directly. 'It was the end of summer when she married him – September, I think. She went to Atlanta, and they were married there, and she never came back. It was just that sudden.' She snapped her fingers. 'Just like that. I saw a picture of him in the paper. Sometimes I think if she'd known how much I loved her – why are there some you can't ever tell? – I think maybe she wouldn't have married; maybe it would've all been different, like I wanted it.' She turned her face into the pillow, and if she cried there was no sound.

On May twentieth she was eighteen; it seemed incredible – Vincent had thought her many years older. He wanted to introduce her at a surprise party, but had finally to admit that this was an unsuitable plan. First off, though the subject was always there on the tip of his tongue, not once had he ever mentioned D. J. to any of his friends; secondly, he could visualize discouragingly well the entertainment provided them at meeting a girl about whom, while they openly shared an apartment, he knew nothing, not even her name. Still the birthday called for some kind of treat. Dinner and the theatre were hopeless. She hadn't, through no fault of his, a dress of any sort. He'd given her forty-odd dollars to buy clothes, and here is what she spent it on: a leather windbreaker, a set of military brushes, a raincoat, a cigarette lighter. Also, her suitcase, which she'd brought to the apartment, had contained nothing but hotel soap, a pair of scissors she used for pruning her hair, two Bibles, and an appalling colour-tinted photograph. The photograph showed a simpering middle-aged woman with dumpy features. There was an inscription: Best Wishes and Good Luck from Martha Lovejoy Hall.

Because she could not cook they had their meals out; his salary and the limitations of her wardrobe confined them mostly to the Automat – her favourite: the macaroni was so delicious! – or one of the bar-grills along Third. And so the birthday dinner was eaten in an Automat. She'd scrubbed her face until the skin shone red, trimmed and shampooed her hair, and with the messy skill of a six-year-old playing grown-up, varnished her nails. She wore the leather windbreaker, and on it pinned a sheaf of violets he'd given her; it must have looked amusing, for two rowdy girls sharing their table giggled frantically. Vincent said if they didn't shut up . . .

'Oh, yeah, who do you think you are?'

'Superman. Jerk thinks he's superman.'

It was too much, and Vincent lost his temper. He shoved back from the table, upsetting a ketchup jar. 'Let's get the hell out of here,' he said, but D. J., who had paid the fracas no attention whatever, went right on spooning blackberry cobbler; furious as he was, he waited quietly until she finished, for he respected her remoteness, and yet wondered in what period of time she lived. It was futile, he'd discovered, to question her past; still, she seemed only now and then aware of the present, and it was likely the future didn't mean much to her. Her mind was like a mirror reflecting blue space in a barren room.

'What would you like now?' he said, as they came into the street. 'We could ride in a cab through the park.'

She wiped off with her jacket-cuff flecks of blackberry staining the corners of her mouth, and said, 'I want to go to a picture show.'

The movies. Again. In the last month he'd seen so many films, snatches of Hollywood dialogue rumbled in his dreams. One Saturday at her insistence they'd bought tickets to three different theatres, cheap places where smells of latrine disinfectant poisoned the air. And each morning before leaving for work he left on the mantel fifty cents – rain or shine, she went to a picture show. But Vincent was sensitive enough to see why: there had been in his own life a certain time of limbo when he'd gone to movies every day, often sitting through several repeats of the same film; it was in its way like religion, for there, watching the shifting patterns of black and white, he knew a release of conscience similar to the kind a man must find confessing to his father.

'Handcuffs,' she said, referring to an incident in *The Thirty-Nine Steps*, which they'd seen at the Beverly in a programme of Hitchcock revivals. 'That blonde woman and the man handcuffed together – well, it made me think of something else.' She stepped into a pair of his pyjamas, pinned the corsage of violets to the edge of her pillow, and folded up on the bed. 'People getting caught like that, locked together.'

Vincent yawned. 'Uh-huh,' he said, and turned off the lights. 'Again, happy birthday darling, it was a happy birthday?'

She said, 'Once I was in this place, and there were two girls dancing; they were so free – there was just them and nobody else, and it was beautiful like a sunset.' She was silent a long while; then, her slow Southern voice dragging over the words: 'It was mighty nice of you to bring me violets.'

'Glad – like them,' he answered sleepily.

'It's a shame they have to die.'

'Yes, well, good night.'

'Good night.'

Close-up. Oh, but John, it isn't for my sake after all we've the children to consider a divorce would ruin their lives!

Fadeout. The screen trembles; rattle of drums, flourish of trumpets: R.K.O. PRESENTS . . .

Here is a hall without exit, a tunnel without end. Overhead, chandeliers sparkle, and wind-bent candles float on currents of air. Before him is an old man rocking in a rocking chair, an old man with yellow-dyed hair, powdered cheeks, kewpie-doll lips: Vincent recognizes Vincent. Go away, screams Vincent, the young and handsome, but Vincent, the old and horrid, creeps forward on all fours, and climbs spiderlike onto his back. Threats, pleas, blows, nothing will dislodge him. And so he races with his shadow, his rider jogging up and down. A serpent of lightning blazes, and all at once the tunnel seethes with men wearing white tie and tails, women costumed in brocaded gowns. He is humiliated; how gauche they must think him appearing at so elegant a gathering carrying on his back, like Sinbad, a sordid old man. The guests stand about in petrified pairs, and there is no conversation. He notices then that many are also saddled with malevolent semblances of themselves, outward embodiments of inner decay. Just beside him a lizard-like man rides an albino-eyed Negro. A man is coming towards him, the host; short, florid, bald, he steps lightly, precisely in glacé shoes; one arm, held stiffly crooked, supports a massive headless hawk whose talons, latched to the wrist, draw blood. The hawk's wings unfurl as its master struts by. On a pedestal there is perched an old-time phonograph. Winding the handle, the host supplies a record: a tinny worn-out waltz vibrates the morning-glory horn. He lifts a hand, and in a soprano voice announces: 'Attention! The dancing will commence.' The host with his hawk weaves in and out as round and round they dip, they turn. The walls widen, the ceiling grows tall. A girl glides into Vincent's arms, and a cracked, imitation of his voice says: 'Lucille, how divine; that exquisite scent, is it violet?' This is Cousin Lucille, and then, as they circle the room, her face changes. Now he waltzes with another. 'Why, Connie, Connie Silver! How marvellous to see you,' shrieks the voice, for Connie is quite deaf. Suddenly a gentleman with a bullet-bashed head cuts in: 'Gordon, forgive me, I never meant. . .' but they are gone, Gordon and Connie, dancing together.

Again, a new partner. It is D. J., and she too has a figure barnacled to her back, an enchanting auburn-haired child; like an emblem of innocence, the child cuddles to her chest a snowball kitten. 'I am heavier than I look,' says the child, and the terrible voice retorts, 'But I am heaviest of all.' The instant their hands meet he begins to feel the weight upon him diminish; the old Vincent is fading. His feet lift off the floor, he floats upward from her embrace. The victrola grinds away loud as ever, but he is rising high, and the white receding faces gleam below like mushrooms on a dark meadow.

The host releases his hawk, sends it soaring. Vincent thinks, no matter, it is a blind thing, and the wicked are safe among the blind. But the hawk wheels above him, swoops down, claws foremost; at last he knows there is to be no freedom.

And the blackness of the room filled his eyes. One arm lolled over the bed's edge, his pillow had fallen to the floor. Instinctively he reached out, asking mother-comfort of the girl beside him. Sheets smooth and cold; emptiness, and the tawdry fragrance of drying voilets. He snapped up straight: 'You, where are you?'

The French doors were open. An ashy trace of moon swayed on the threshold, for it was not yet light, and in the kitchen the refrigerator purred like a giant cat. A stack of papers rustled on the desk. Vincent called again, softly this time, as if he wished himself unheard. Rising, he stumbled forward on dizzy legs, and looked into the yard. She was there, leaning, half-kneeling, against the heaven tree. 'What?' and she whirled around. He could not see her well, only a dark substantial shape. She came closer. A finger pressed her lips.

'What is it?' he whispered.

She rose on tiptoe, and her breath tingled in his ear. 'I warn you, go inside.'

'Stop this foolishness,' he said in a normal voice. 'Out here barefooted, you'll catch . . .' but she clamped a hand over his mouth.

'I saw him,' she whispered. 'He's here.'

Vincent knocked her hand away. It was hard not to slap her. 'Him! Him! Him! What's the matter with you? Are you –' he tried too late to prevent the word – 'crazy?' There, the acknowledgement of something he'd known, but had not allowed his conscious mind to crystallize. And he thought: Why should this make a difference? A man cannot be held to account for those he loves. Untrue. Feeble-witted Lucille weaving mosaics on silk, embroidering his name on scarves; Connie, in her hushed deaf world, listening for his footstep, a sound she would surely hear; Allen T. Baker thumbing his photograph, still needing love, but old now, and lost – all betrayed. And he'd betrayed himself with talents unexploited, voyages never taken, promises unfulfilled. There had seemed nothing left him until – oh, why in his lovers must he always find the broken image of himself? Now, as he looked at her in the ageing dawn, his heart was cold with the death of love.

She moved away, and under the tree. 'Leave me here,' she said, her eyes scanning tenement windows. 'Only a moment.'

Vincent waited, waited. On all sides windows looked down like the doors of dreams, and overhead, four flights up, a family's laundry whipped a washline. The setting moon was like the early moon of dusk, a vapourish cartwheel, and the sky, draining of dark, was washed with grey. Sunrise wind shook the leaves of the heaven tree, and in the paling light the yard assumed a pattern, objects a position, and from the roofs came the throaty morning rumble of pigeons. A light went on. Another.

And at last she lowered her head; whatever she was looking for, she had not found it. Or, he wondered as she turned to him with tilted lips, had she?

'Well, you're home kinda early, aren't you, Mr Waters?' It was Mrs Brennan, the super's bowlegged wife. 'And, well, Mr Waters – lovely weather, aint it? – you and me got sumpin' to talk about.'

'Mrs Brennan –' how hard it was to breathe, to speak; the words grated his hurting throat, sounded loud as thunderclaps – 'I'm rather ill, so if you don't mind ...' and he tried to brush past her.

'Say, that's a pity. Ptomaine, must be ptomaine. Yessir, I tell you a person can't be too careful. It's them Jews, you know. They run all them delicatessens. Uh uh, none of that Jew food for me.' She stepped before the gate, blocking his path, and pointed an admonishing finger : 'Trouble with you, Mr Waters, is that you don't lead no kinda *normal* life.'

A knot of pain was set like a malignant jewel in the core of his head ; each aching motion made jewelled pinpoints of colour flare out. The super's wife blabbed on, but there were blank moments when, fortunately, he could not hear at all. It was like a radio – the volume turned low, then full blast. 'Now I know she's a decent Christian lady, Mr Waters, or else what would a gentleman like you be doing with – hm. Still, the fact is, Mr Cooper don't tell lies, and he's a real calm man, besides. Been gas meter man for this district I don't know how long.' A truck rolled down the street spraying water, and her voice, submerged below its roar, came up again like a shark. 'Mr Cooper had every reason to believe she meant to kill him – well, you can imagine, her standin' there with them scissors, and shoutin'. She called him an Eyetalian name. Now all you got to do is look at Mr Cooper to know he ain't no Eyetalian. Well, you can see, Mr Waters, such carryings-on are bound to give the house a bad ...'

Brittle sunshine plundering the depths of his eyes made tears, and the super's wife, wagging her finger, seemed to break into separate pieces : a nose, a chin, a red, red eye. 'Mr Destronelli,' he said. 'Excuse me, Mrs Brennan, I mean excuse me.' She thinks I'm drunk, and I'm sick, and can't she see I'm sick? 'My guest is leaving. She's leaving today, and she won't be back.'

'Well, now, you don't say,' said Mrs Brennan, clucking her tongue. 'Looks like she needs a rest, poor little thing. So pale, sorta. Course I don't want no more to do with them Eyetalians than the next one, but imagine thinking Mr Cooper was an Eyetalian. Why, he's white as you or me.' She tapped his shoulder solicitously. 'Sorry you feel so sick, Mr Waters; ptomaine, I tell you. A person can't be too care . . .'

The hall smelled of cooking and incinerator ashes. There was a stairway which he never used, his apartment being on the first floor, straight ahead. A match snapped fire, and Vincent, groping his way, saw a small boy – he was not more than three or four – squatting under the stairwell; he was playing with a big box of kitchen matches, and Vincent's presence appeared not to interest him. He simply struck another match. Vincent could not make his mind work well enough to phrase a reprimand, and as he waited there, tongue-tied, a door, his door, opened.

Hide. For if she saw him she would know something was wrong, suspect something. And if she spoke, if their eyes met, then he would never be able to go through with it. So he pressed into a dark corner behind the little boy, and the little boy said, 'Whatcha doin', Mister?' She was coming – he heard the slap of her sandals, the green whisper of her raincoat. 'Whatcha doin', Mister?' Quickly, his heart banging in his chest, Vincent stooped and, squeezing the child against him, pressed his hand over its mouth so it could not make a sound. He did not see her pass; it was later, after the front door clicked, that he realized she was gone. The little boy sank back on the floor. 'Whatcha doin', Mister?'

Four aspirins, one right after the other, and he came back into the room; the bed had not been tidied for a week, a spilt ash-tray messed the floor, odds and ends of clothing decorated improbable places, lampshades and such. But tomorrow, if he felt better, there would be a general cleaning; perhaps he'd have the walls repainted, maybe fix up the yard. Tomorrow he could begin thinking about his friends again, accept invitations, entertain. And yet this prospect, tasted in advance, was without flavour: all he'd known before seemed to him now sterile and spurious. Footsteps in the hall; could she return this soon, the movie over, the afternoon gone? Fever can make time pass so queerly, and for an instant he felt as though his bones were floating loose inside him. Clopclop, a child's sloppy shoe-fall, the footsteps passed up the stairs, and Vincent moved, floated towards the mirrored closet. He longed to hurry, knowing he must, but the air seemed thick with gummy fluid. He brought her suitcase from the closet, and put it on the bed, a sad cheap suitcase with rusty locks and a warped hide. He eyed it with guilt. Where would she go? How would she live? When he'd broken with Connie, Gordon, all the others, there had been about it at least a certain dignity. Really, though – and he'd thought it out – there was no other way. So he gathered her belongings. Miss Martha Lovejoy Hall peeked out from under the leather windbreaker, her music-teacher's face smiling an oblique reproach. Vincent turned her over, face down, and tucked in the frame an envelope containing twenty dollars. That would buy a ticket back to Glass Hill, or wherever it was she came from. Now he tried to close the case, and, too weak with fever, collapsed on the bed. Quick yellow wings glided through the window. A butterfly. He'd never seen a butterfly in this city, and it was like a floating mysterious flower, like a sign of some sort, and he watched with a kind of horror as it waltzed in the air. Outside, somewhere, the razzle-dazzle of a beggar's grind-organ started up; it sounded like a broken-down pianola, and it played *La Marseillaise*. The butterfly lighted on her painting, crept across crystal eyes, and flattened its wings like a ribbon bow over the loose head. He fished about in the suitcase until he found her scissors. He first purposed to slash the butterfly's wings, but it spiralled to the ceiling and hung there like a star. The scissors stabbed the hawk's heart, ate through canvas like a ravening steel mouth, scraps of picture flaking the floor like cuttings of stiff hair. He went on his knees, pushed the pieces into a pile, put them in the suitcase, and slammed the lid shut. He was crying. And through the tears the butterfly magnified on the ceiling, huge as a bird, and there was more: a flock of lilting, winking yellow; whispering lonesomely, like surf sucking a shore. The wind from their wings blew the room into space. He heaved forward, the suitcase banging his leg, and threw open the door. A match flared. The little boy said: 'Whatcha doin', Mister?' And Vincent, setting the suitcase in the hall, grinned sheepishly. He closed the door like a thief, bolted the safety lock and, pulling up a chair, tilted it under the knob. In the still room there was only the subtlety of shifting sunlight and a crawling butterfly; it drifted downward like a tricky scrap of crayon paper, and landed on a candlestick. *Sometimes he is not a man at all –* she'd told him that, huddling here on the bed, talking swiftly in the minutes before dawn – *sometimes he is something very different: a hawk, a child, a butterfly.* And then she'd said: *At the place where they took me there were hundreds of old ladies, and young men, and one of the young men said he was a pirate, and one of the old ladies – she was near ninety – used to make me feel her stomach. 'Feel,' she'd say, 'feel how strong he kicks?' This old lady took painting class, too, and her paintings looked like crazy quilts. And naturally he was in this place. Mr Destronelli. Only he called himself Gum. Doctor Gum. Oh, he didn't fool me, even though he wore a grey wig, and made himself up to look real old and kind, I knew. And then one day I left, ran clear away, and hid under a lilac bush, and a man came along in a little red car, and he had a little mouse-haired moustache, and little cruel eyes. But it was him. And when I told him who he was he made me get out of his car. And then another man, that was in Philadelphia, picked me up in a café and took me into an alley. He talked Italian, and had tattoo pictures all over. But it was him. And the next man, he was the one who painted his toenails, sat down beside me in a movie because he thought I was a boy, and when he found out I wasn't he didn't get mad but let me live in his room, and cooked pretty things for me to eat. But he wore a silver locket and one day I looked inside and there was a picture of Miss Hall. So I knew it was him, so I had this feeling she was dead, so I knew he was going to murder me. And he will. He will.'* Dusk, and nightfall, and the fibres of sound called silence wove a shiny blue mask. Waking, he peered through eyeslits, heard the frenzied pulse-beat of his watch, the scratch of a key in a lock. Somewhere in this dusk a murderer separates himself from shadow and with a rope follows the flash of silk legs up doomed stairs. And here the dreamer staring through his mask dreams of deceit. Without investigating he knows the suitcase is missing, that she has come, that she has gone; why, then, does he feel so little the pleasure of safety, and only cheated, and small – small as the night when he searched the moon through an old man's telescope?

3

Like fragments of an old letter, scattered popcorn lay trampled flat, and she, leaning back in a watchman's attitude, allowed her gaze to hunt among it, as if deciphering here and there a word, an answer. Her eyes shifted discreetly to the man mounting the steps, Vincent. There was about him the freshness of a shower, shave, cologne, but dreary blue circled his eyes, and the crisp seersucker into which he'd changed had been made for a heavier man: a long month of pneumonia, and wakeful burning nights had lightened his weight a dozen pounds, and more. Each morning, evening, meeting her here at his gate, or near the gallery, or outside the restaurant where he lunched, a nameless disorder took hold, a paralysis of time and identity. The wordless pantomime of her pursuit contracted his heart, and there were coma-like days when she seemed not one, but all, a multiple person, and her shadow in the street every shadow, following and followed. And once they'd been alone together in an automatic elevator, and he'd screamed: 'I am not him! Only me, only me!' But she smiled as she'd smiled telling of the man with painted toenails, because, after all, she knew.

It was suppertime, and, not knowing where to eat, he paused under a street lamp that, blooming abruptly, fanned complex light over stone; while he waited there came a clap of thunder, and all along the street every face but two, his and the girl's, tilted upward. A blast of river breeze tossed the children's laughter as they, linking arms, pranced like carousel ponies, and carried the mama's voice who, leaning from a window, howled: rain, Rachel, rain – gonna rain gonna rain! And the gladiola, ivy-filled flower cart jerked crazily as the peddler, one eye slanted skyward, raced for shelter. A potted geranium fell off, and the little girls gathered the blooms and tucked them behind their ears. The blending spatter of running feet and raindrops tinkled on the xylophone sidewalks – the slamming of doors, the lowering of windows, then nothing but silence, and rain. Presently, with slow scraping steps, she came below the lamp to stand beside him, and it was as if the sky were a thunder-cracked mirror, for the rain fell between them like a curtain of splintered glass.

My Side of the Matter

I know what is being said about me and you can take my side or theirs, that's your own business. It's my word against Eunice's and Olivia-Ann's, and it should be plain enough to anyone with two good eyes which one of us has their wits about them. I just want the citizens of the U.S.A. to know the facts, that's all.

The facts: On Sunday, 12 August, this year of our Lord, Eunice tried to kill me with her papa's Civil War sword and Olivia-Ann cut up all over the place with a fourteen-inch hog knife. This is not even to mention lots of other things.

It began six months ago when I married Marge. That was the first thing I did wrong. We were married in Mobile after an acquaintance of only four days. We were both sixteen and she was visiting my cousin Georgia. Now that I've had plenty of time to think it over, I can't for the life of me figure how I fell for the likes of her. She has no looks, no body, and no brains whatsoever. But Marge is a natural blonde and maybe that's the answer. Well, we were married going on three months when Marge ups and gets pregnant; the second thing I did wrong. Then she starts hollering that she's got to go home to Mama – only she hasn't got no mama, just these two aunts. Eunice and Olivia-Ann. So she makes me quit my perfectly swell position clerking at the Cash'n' Carry and move here to Admiral's Mill which is nothing but a damn gap in the road any way you care to consider it.

The day Marge and I got off the train at the L&N depot it was raining cats and dogs and do you think anyone came to meet us? I'd shelled out forty-one cents for a telegram, too! Here my wife's pregnant and we have to tramp seven miles in a downpour. It was bad on Marge as I couldn't carry hardly any of our stuff on account of I have terrible trouble with my back. When I first caught sight of this house I must say I was impressed. It's big and yellow and has real columns out in front and japonica trees, both red and white, lining the yard.

Eunice and Olivia-Ann had seen us coming and were waiting in the hall. I swear I wish you could get a look at these two. Honest, you'd die! Eunice is this big old fat thing with a behind that must weigh a tenth of a ton. She troops around the house, rain or shine, in this real old-fashioned nighty, calls it a kimono, but it isn't anything in this world but a dirty flannel nighty. Furthermore she chews tobacco and tries to pretend so ladylike, spitting on the sly. She keeps gabbing about what a fine education she had, which is her way of attempting to make me feel bad, although, personally, it never bothers me so much as one whit as I know for a fact she can't even read the funnies without she spells out every single, solitary word. You've got to hand her one thing, though – she can add and subtract money so fast that there's no doubt but what she could be up in Washington, D.C., working where they make the stuff. Not that she hasn't got plenty of money! Naturally she says she hasn't but I know she has because one day, accidentally, I happened to find close to a thousand dollars hidden in a flower pot on the side porch. I didn't touch one cent, only Eunice says I stole a hundred-dollar bill which is a venomous lie from start to finish. Of course anything Eunice says is an order from headquarters as not a breathing soul in Admiral's Mill can stand up and say he doesn't owe her money and if she said Charlie Carson (a blind, ninety-year-old invalid who hasn't taken a step since 1896) threw her on her back and raped her everybody in this county would swear the same on a stack of Bibles.

Now Olivia-Ann is worse, and that's the truth! Only she's not so bad on the nerves as Eunice, for she is a natural-born half-wit and ought really to be kept in somebody's attic. She's real pale and skinny and has a moustache. She squats around most of the time whittling on a stick with her fourteen-inch hog knife, otherwise she's up to some devilment, like what she did to Mrs Harry Steller Smith. I swore not ever to tell anyone that, but when a vicious attempt has been made on a person's life, I say the hell with promises.

Mrs Harry Stella Smith was Eunice's canary named after a woman from Pensacola who makes home-made cure-all that Eunice takes for the gout. One day I heard this terrible racket in the parlour and upon investigating, what did I find but Olivia-Ann shooing Mrs Harry Steller Smith out an open window with a broom and the door to the bird cage wide. If I hadn't walked in at exactly that moment she might never have been caught. She got scared that I would tell Eunice and blurted out the whole thing, said it wasn't fair to keep one of God's creatures locked up that way, besides which she couldn't stand Mrs Harry Steller Smith's singing. Well, I felt kind of sorry for her and she gave me two dollars, so I helped her cook up a story for Eunice. Of course I wouldn't have taken the money except I thought it would ease her conscience.

The very *first* words Eunice said when I stepped inside this house were, 'So this is what you ran off behind our back and married, Marge?'

Marge says, 'Isn't he the best-looking thing, Aunt Eunice?'

Eunice eyes me u-p and d-o-w-n and says, 'Tell him to turn around.'

While my back is turned, Eunice says, 'You sure must've picked the runt of the litter. Why, this isn't any sort of man at all.'

I've never been so taken back in my life! True, I'm slightly stocky, but then I haven't got my full growth yet.

'He is too,' says Marge.

Olivia-Ann, who's been standing there with her mouth so wide the flies could buzz in and out, says, 'You heard what Sister said. He's not any sort of a man whatsoever. The very idea of this little runt running around claiming to be a man! Why, he isn't even of the male sex!'

Marge says, 'You seem to forget, Aunt Olivia-Ann, that this is my husband, the father of my unborn child.'

Eunice made a nasty sound like only she can and said, 'Well, all I can say is I most certainly wouldn't be bragging about it.'

Isn't that a nice welcome? And after I gave up my perfectly swell position clerking at the Cash'n' Carry.

But it's not a drop in the bucket to what came later that same evening. After Bluebell cleared away the supper dishes, Marge asked, just as nice as she could, if we could borrow the car and drive over to the picture show at Phoenix City.

'You must be clear out of your head,' says Eunice, and, honest, you'd think we'd asked for the kimono off her back.

'You must be clear out of your head,' says Olivia-Ann.

'It's six o'clock,' says Eunice, 'and if you think I'd let that runt drive my just-as-good-as-brand-new 1934 Chevrolet as far as the privy and back you must've gone clear out of your head.'

Naturally such language makes Marge cry.

'Never you mind, honey,' I said, 'I've driven pulenty of Cadillacs in my time.'

'Humf,' says Eunice.

'Yeah,' says I.

Eunice says, 'If he's ever so much as driven a plough I'll eat a dozen gophers fried in turpentine.'

'I won't have you refer to my husband in any such manner,' says Marge. 'You're acting simply outlandish! Why, you'd think I'd picked up some absolutely strange man in some absolutely strange place.'

'If the shoe fits, wear it!' says Eunice.

'Don't think you can pull the sheep over our eyes,' says Olivia-Ann in that braying voice of hers so much like the mating call of a jackass you can't rightly tell the difference.

'We weren't born just around the corner, you know,' says Eunice.

Marge says, 'I'll give you to understand that I'm legally wed till death do us part to this man by a certified justice of the peace as of three and one-half months ago. Ask anybody. Furthermore, Aunt Eunice, he is free, white and sixteen. Furthermore, George Far Sylvester does not appreciate hearing his father referred to in any such manner.'

George Far Sylvester is the name we've planned for the baby. Has a strong sound, don't you think? Only the way things stand I have positively no feelings in the matter now whatsoever.

'How can a girl have a baby with a girl?' says Olivia-Ann, which was a calculated attack on my manhood. 'I do declare there's something new every day.'

'Oh, shush up,' says Eunice. 'Let us hear no more about the picture show in Phoenix City.'

Marge sobs, 'Oh-h-h, but it's Judy Garland.'

'Never mind, honey,' I said, 'I most likely saw the show in Mobile ten years ago.'

'That's a deliberate falsehood,' shouts Olivia-Ann. 'Oh, you are a scoundrel, you are. Judy hasn't been in the pictures ten years.' Olivia-Ann's never seen not even one picture show in her entire fifty-two years (she won't tell anybody how old she is but I dropped a card to the capitol in Montgomery and they were very nice about answering), but she subscribes to eight movie books. According to Postmistress Delancey, it's the only mail she ever gets outside of the Sears & Roebuck. She has this positively morbid crush on Gary Cooper and has one trunk and two suitcases full of his photos.

So we got up from the table and Eunice lumbers over to the window and looks out to the chinaberry tree and says, 'Birds settling in their roost – time we went to bed. You have your old room, Marge, and I've fixed a cot for this gentleman on the back porch.'

It took a solid minute for that to sink in.

I said, 'And what, if I'm not too bold to ask, is the objection to my sleeping with my lawful wife?'

Then they both started yelling at me.

So Marge threw a conniption fit right then and there. 'Stop it, stop it, stop it! I can't stand any more. Go on, babydoll – go on and sleep where they say. Tomorrow we'll see. . . .'

Eunice says, 'I swanee if the child hasn't got a grain of sense, after all.'

'Poor dear,' says Olivia-Ann, wrapping her arm around Marge's waist and herding her off, 'poor dear, so young, so innocent. Let's us just go and have a good cry on Olivia-Ann's shoulder.'

May, June, and July and the best part of August I've squatted and sweltered on that damn back porch without an ounce of screening. And Marge – she hasn't opened her mouth in protest, not once! This part of Alabama is swampy, with mosquitoes that could murder a buffalo, given half a chance, not to mention dangerous flying roaches and a posse of local rats big enough to haul a wagon train from here to Timbuctoo. Oh, if it wasn't for that little unborn George I would've been making dust tracks on the road, way before now. I mean to say I haven't had five seconds alone with Marge since that first night. One or the other is always chaperoning and last week they like to have blown their tops when Marge locked herself in her room and they couldn't find me nowhere. The truth is I'd been down watching the niggers bale cotton but just for spite I let on to Eunice like Marge and I'd been up to no good. After that they added Bluebell to the shift.

And all this time I haven't even had cigarette change.

Eunice has hounded me day in and day out about getting a job. 'Why don't the little heathen go out and get some honest work?' says she. As you've probably noticed, she never speaks to me directly, though more often than not I am the only one in her royal presence. 'If he was any sort of man you could call a man he'd be trying to put a crust of bread in that girl's mouth instead of stuffing his own off my vittles.' I think you should know that I've been living almost exclusively on cold yams and leftover grits for three months and thirteen days and I've been down to consult Dr A. N. Carter twice. He's not exactly sure whether I have the scurvy or not.

And as for my not working, I'd like to know what a man of my abilities, a man who held a perfectly swell position with the Cash'n' Carry would find to do in a flea-bag like Admiral's Mill? There is all of one store here and Mr Tubberville, the proprietor, is actually so lazy it's painful for him to have to sell anything. Then we have the Morning Star Baptist Church but they already have a preacher, an awful old turd named Shell whom Eunice drug over one day to see about the salvation of my soul. I heard him with my own ears tell her I was too far gone.

But it's what Eunice has done to Marge that really takes the cake. She has turned that girl against me in the most villainous fashion that words could not describe. Why, she even reached the point when she was sassing me back, but I provided her with a couple of good slaps and put a stop to that. No wife of mine is ever going to be disrespectful to me, not on your life!

The enemy lines are stretched tight: Bluebell, Olivia-Ann, Eunice, Marge, and the whole rest of Admiral's Mill (pop. 342). Allies: none. Such was the situation as of Sunday, 11 August, when the attempt was made upon my very life.

Yesterday was quiet and hot enough to melt rock. The trouble began at exactly two o'clock. I know because Eunice has one of those fool cuckoo contraptions and it scares the daylights out of me. I was minding my own personal business in the parlour, composing a song on the upright piano which Eunice bought for Olivia-Ann and hired a teacher to come all the way from Columbus, Georgia, once a week. Postmistress Delancey, who was my friend till she decided that it was maybe not so wise, says that the fancy teacher tore out of this house one afternoon like old Adolf Hitler was on his tail and leaped in his Ford coupé, never to be heard from again. Like I say, I'm trying to keep cool in the parlour not bothering a living soul when Olivia-Ann trots in with her hair all twisted up in curlers and shrieks, 'Cease that infernal racket this very instant! Can't you give a body a minute's rest? And get off my piano right smart. It's not your piano, it's my piano and if you don't get off it right smart I'll have you in court like a shot the first Monday in September.'

She's not anything in this world but jealous on account of I'm a natural-born musician and the songs I make up out of my own head are absolutely marvellous.

'And just look what you've done to my genuine ivory keys, Mr Sylvester,' says she, trotting over to the piano, 'torn nearly every one of them off right at the roots for purentee meanness, that's what you've done.'

She knows good and well that the piano was ready for the junk heap the moment I entered this house.

I said, 'Seeing as you're such a know-it-all, Miss Olivia-Ann, maybe it would interest you to know that I'm in the possession of a few interesting tales myself. A few things that maybe other people would be very grateful to know. Like what happened to Mrs Harry Steller Smith, as for instance.'

Remember Mrs Harry Steller Smith?

She paused and looked at the empty bird cage. 'You gave me your oath,' says she and turned the most terrifying shade of purple.

'Maybe I did and again maybe I didn't,' says I. 'You did an evil thing when you betrayed Eunice that way but if some people will leave other people alone then maybe I can overlook it.'

Well, sir, she walked out of there just as *nice* and *quiet* as you please. So I went and stretched out on the sofa which is the most horrible piece of furniture I've ever seen and is part of a matched set Eunice bought in Atlanta in 1912 and paid two thousand dollars for, cash – or so she claims. This set is black and olive plush and smells like wet chicken feathers on a damp day. There is a big table in one corner of the parlour which supports two pictures of Miss E and O-A's mama and papa. Papa is kind of handsome but just between you and me I'm convinced he has black blood in him from somewhere. He was a captain in the Civil War and that is one thing I'll never forget on account of his sword which is displayed over the mantel and figures prominently in the action yet to come. Mama has that hang-dog, half-wit look like Olivia-Ann, though I must say Mama carries it better.

So I had just dozed off when I heard Eunice bellowing, 'Where is he? Where is he?' And the next thing I know she's framed in the doorway with her hands planted plumb on those hippo hips and the whole pack scrunched up behind her : Bluebell, Olivia-Ann and Marge.

Several seconds passed with Eunice tapping her big old bare foot just as fast and furious as she could and fanning her fat face with this cardboard picture of Niagara Falls.

'Where is it?' says she. 'Where's my hundred dollars that he made away with while my trusting back was turned?'

'*This* is the straw that broke the camel's back,' says I, but I was too hot and tired to get up.

'That's not the only back that's going to be broke,' says she, her bug eyes about to pop clear out of their sockets. 'That was my funeral money and I want it back. Wouldn't you know he'd steal from the dead?'

'Maybe he didn't take it,' says Marge.

'You keep your mouth out of this, missy,' says Olivia-Ann.

'He stole my money sure as shooting,' says Eunice. 'Why, look at his eyes – black with guilt!'

I yawned and said, 'Like they say in the courts – if the party of the first part falsely accuses the party of the second part then the party of the first part can be locked away in jail even if the State Home is where they rightfully belong for the protection of all concerned.'

'God will punish him,' says Eunice.

'Oh, Sister,' says Olivia-Ann, 'let us not wait for God.'

Whereupon Eunice advances on me with this most peculiar look, her dirty flannel nighty jerking along the floor. And Olivia-Ann leeches after her and Bluebell lets forth this moan that must have been heard clear to Eufala and back while Marge stands there wringing her hands and whimpering.

'Oh-h-h,' sobs Marge, 'please give her back that money, babydoll.'

I said, 'et tu Brute?' which is from William Shakespeare.

'Look at the likes of him,' says Eunice, 'lying around all day not doing so much as licking a postage stamp.'

'Pitiful,' clucks Olivia-Ann.

'You'd think he was having a baby instead of that poor child.' Eunice speaking.

Bluebell tosses in her two cents, 'Ain't it the truth?'

'Well, if it isn't the old pots calling the kettle black,' says I.

'After loafing here for three months does this runt have the audacity to cast aspersions in my direction?' says Eunice.

I merely flicked a bit of ash from my sleeve and not the least bit fazed said, 'Dr A. N. Carter has informed me that I am in a dangerous scurvy condition and can't stand the least excitement whatsoever – otherwise I'm liable to foam at the mouth and bite somebody.'

Then Bluebell says, 'Why don't he go back to that trash in Mobile, Miss Eunice? I'se sick and tired of carryin' his ol' slop jar.'

Naturally that coal-black nigger made me so mad I couldn't see straight.

So just as calm as a cucumber I arose and picked up this umbrella off the hat tree and rapped her across the head with it until it cracked smack in two.

'My real Japanese silk parasol!' shrieks Olivia-Ann.

Marge cries, 'You've killed Bluebell, you've killed poor old Bluebell!'

Eunice shoves Olivia-Ann and says, 'He's gone clear out of his head, Sister! Run! Run and get Mr Tubberville!'

'I don't like Mr Tubberville,' says Olivia-Ann staunchly. 'I'll go get my hog knife.' And she makes a dash for the door but seeing as I care nothing for death I brought her down with a sort of tackle. It wrenched my back something terrible.

'He's going to kill her!' hollers Eunice loud enough to bring the house down. 'He's going to murder us all! I warned you, Marge. Quick, child, get Papa's sword!'

So Marge gets Papa's sword and hands it to Eunice. Talk about wifely devotion! And, if that's not bad enough, Olivia-Ann gives me this terrific knee punch and I had to let go. The next thing you know we hear her out in the yard bellowing hymns.

> Mine eyes have seen the glory of the
> coming of the Lord;
> He is trampling out the vintage where
> the grapes of wrath are stored. . . .

Meanwhile Eunice is sashaying all over the place wildly thrashing Papa's sword and somehow I've managed to clamber atop the piano. Then Eunice climbs up on the piano stool and how that rickety contraption survived a monster like her I'll never be the one to tell.

'Come down from there, you yellow coward, before I run

you through,' says she and takes a whack and I've got a half-inch cut to prove it.

By this time Bluebell has recovered and skittered away to join Olivia-Ann holding services in the front yard. I guess they were expecting my body and God knows it would've been theirs if Marge hadn't passed out cold.

That's the only good thing I've got to say for Marge.

What happened after that I can't rightly remember except for Olivia-Ann reappearing with her fourteen-inch hog knife and a bunch of the neighbours. But suddenly Marge was the star attraction and I suppose they carried her to her room. Anyway, as soon as they left I barricaded the parlour door.

I've got all those black and olive plush chairs pushed against it and that big mahogany table that must weigh a couple of tons and the hat tree and lots of other stuff. I've locked the windows and pulled down the shades. Also I've found a five-pound box of Sweet Love candy and this very minute I'm munching a juicy, creamy, chocolate cherry. Sometimes they come to the door and knock and yell and plead. Oh, yes, they've started singing a song of a very different colour. But as for me – I give them a tune on the piano every now and then just to let them know I'm cheerful.

A Tree of Night

It was winter. A string of naked light bulbs, from which it seemed all warmth had been drained, illuminated the little depot's cold, windy platform. Earlier in the evening it had rained, and now icicles hung along the station-house eaves like some crystal monster's vicious teeth. Except for a girl, young and rather tall, the platform was deserted. The girl wore a grey flannel suit, a raincoat, and a plaid scarf. Her hair, parted in the middle and rolled up neatly on the sides, was rich blondish-brown; and, while her face tended to be too thin and narrow, she was, though not extraordinarily so, attractive. In addition to an assortment of magazines and a grey suede purse on which elaborate brass letters spelled Kay, she carried conspicuously a green Western guitar.

When the train, spouting steam and glaring with light, came out of the darkness and rumbled to a halt, Kay assembled her paraphernalia and climbed up into the last coach.

The coach was a relic with a decaying interior of ancient red-plush seats, bald in spots, and peeling iodine-coloured woodwork. An old-time copper lamp, attached to the ceiling, looked romantic and out of place. Gloomy dead smoke sailed the air; and the car's heated closeness accentuated the stale odour of discarded sandwiches, apple cores, and orange hulls: this garbage, including Lily cups, soda-pop bottles, and mangled newspapers, littered the long aisle. From a water cooler, embedded in the wall, a steady stream trickled to the floor. The passengers, who glanced up wearily when Kay entered, were not, it seemed, at all conscious of any discomfort.

Kay resisted a temptation to hold her nose and threaded her way carefully down the aisle, tripping once, without disaster, over a dozing fat man's protruding leg. Two nondescript men turned an interested eye as she passed; and a kid stood up in his seat squalling, 'Hey, Mama, look at de banjo! Hey, lady, lemme play ya banjo!' till a slap from Mama quelled him.

There was only one empty place. She found it at the end of the car in an isolated alcove occupied already by a man and woman who were sitting with their feet settled lazily on the vacant seat opposite. Kay hesitated a second then said, 'Would you mind if I sat here?'

The woman's head snapped up as if she had not been asked a simple question, but stabbed with a needle, too. Nevertheless, she managed a smile. 'Can't say as I see what's to stop you, honey,' she said, taking her feet down and also, with a curious impersonality, removing the feet of the man who was staring out the window, paying no attention whatsoever.

Thanking the woman, Kay took off her coat, sat down, and arranged herself with purse and guitar at her side, magazines in her lap: comfortable enough, though she wished she had a pillow for her back.

The train lurched; a ghost of steam hissed against the window; slowly the dingy lights of the lonesome depot faded past.

'Boy, what a jerkwater dump,' said the woman. 'No town, no nothin'.'

Kay said, 'The town's a few miles away.'

'That so? Live there?'

No. Kay explained she had been at the funeral of an uncle. An uncle who, though she did not of course mention it, had left her nothing in his will but the green guitar. Where was she going? Oh, back to college.

After mulling this over, the woman concluded, 'What'll you ever learn in a place like that? Let me tell you, honey, I'm plenty educated and I never saw the inside of no college.'

'You didn't?' murmured Kay politely and dismissed the matter by opening one of her magazines. The light was dim for reading and none of the stories looked in the least compelling. However, not wanting to become involved in a conversational marathon, she continued gazing at it stupidly till she felt a furtive tap on her knee.

'Don't read,' said the woman. 'I need somebody to talk to.

Naturally, it's no fun talking to *him*.' She jerked a thumb towards the silent man. 'He's afflicted: deaf and dumb, know what I mean?'

Kay closed the magazine and looked at her more or less for the first time. She was short; her feet barely scraped the floor. And like many undersized people she had a freak of structure, in her case an enormous, really huge head. Rouge so brightened her sagging, flesh-featured face it was difficult even to guess at her age: perhaps fifty, fifty-five. Her big sheep eyes squinted, as if distrustful of what they saw. Her hair was an obviously dyed red, and twisted into parched, fat corkscrew curls. A once-elegant lavender hat of impressive size flopped crazily on the side of her head, and she was kept busy brushing back a drooping cluster of celluloid cherries sewed to the brim. She wore a plain, somewhat shabby blue dress. Her breath had a vividly sweetish gin smell.

'You do wanna talk to me, don't you honey?'

'Sure,' said Kay, moderately amused.

'Course you do. You bet you do. That's what I like about a train. Bus people are a close-mouthed buncha dopes. But a train's the place for putting your cards on the table, that's what I always say.' Her voice was cheerful and booming, husky as a man's. 'But on accounta *him*, I always try to get us this here seat; it's more private, like a swell compartment, see?'

'It's very pleasant,' Kay agreed. 'Thanks for letting me join you.'

'Only too glad to. We don't have much company; it makes some folks nervous to be around him.'

As if to deny it, the man made a queer, furry sound deep in his throat and plucked the woman's sleeve. 'Leave me alone, dear-heart,' she said, as if she were talking to an inattentive child. 'I'm O.K. We're just having us a nice little ol' talk. Now behave yourself or this pretty girl will go away. She's very rich; she goes to college.' And winking, she added, 'He thinks I'm drunk.'

The man slumped in the seat, swung his head sideways, and studied Kay intently from the corners of his eyes. These eyes, like a pair of clouded milky-blue marbles, were thickly lashed and oddly beautiful. Now, except for a certain remoteness, his wide, hairless face had no real expression. It was as if he were incapable of experiencing or reflecting the slightest emotion. His grey hair was clipped close and combed forward into uneven bangs. He looked like a child aged abruptly by some uncanny method. He wore a frayed blue serge suit, and he had anointed himself with a cheap, vile perfume. Around his wrist was strapped a Mickey Mouse watch.

'He thinks I'm drunk,' the woman repeated. 'And the real funny part is, I am. Oh shoot – you gotta do something, ain't that right?' She bent closer. 'Say, ain't it?'

Kay was still gawking at the man; the way he was looking at her made her squeamish, but she could not take her eyes off him. 'I guess so,' she said.

'Then let's us have us a drink,' suggested the woman. She plunged her hand into an oilcloth satchel and pulled out a partially filled gin bottle. She began to unscrew the cap, but, seeming to think better of this, handed the bottle to Kay. 'Gee, I forgot about you being company,' she said. 'I'll go get us some nice paper cups.'

So, before Kay could protest that she did not want a drink, the woman had risen and started none too steadily down the aisle towards the water cooler.

Kay yawned and rested her forehead against the windowpane, her fingers idly strumming the guitar: the strings sang a hollow, lulling tune, as monotonously soothing as the Southern landscape, smudged in darkness, flowing past the window. An icy winter moon rolled above the train across the night sky like a thin white wheel.

And then, without warning, a strange thing happened: the man reached out and gently stroked Kay's cheek. Despite the breathtaking delicacy of this movement, it was such a bold gesture Kay was at first too startled to know what to make of it: her thoughts shot in three or four fantastic directions. He leaned forward till his queer eyes were very near her own; the reek of his perfume was sickening. The guitar was silent while they exchanged a searching gaze. Suddenly, from some spring of compassion, she felt for him a keen sense of pity; but also, and this she could not suppress, an overpowering disgust, an absolute loathing: something about him, an elusive quality she could not quite put a finger on, reminded her of – of what?

After a little, he lowered his hand solemnly and sank back in the seat, an asinine grin transfiguring his face, as if he had performed a clever stunt for which he wished applause.

'Giddyup! Giddup! my little bucker-ROOS . . .' shouted the woman. And she sat down, loudly proclaiming to be, 'Dizzy as a witch! Dog tired! Whew!' From a handful of Lily cups she separated two and casually thrust the rest down her blouse. 'Keep 'em safe and dry, ha ha ha. . . .' A coughing spasm seized her, but when it was over she appeared calmer. 'Has my boy friend been entertaining?' she asked, patting her bosom reverently. 'Ah, he's so sweet.' She looked as if she might pass out. Kay rather wished she would.

'I don't want a drink,' Kay said, returning the bottle. 'I never drink: I hate the taste.'

'Mustn't be a kill-joy,' said the woman firmly. 'Here now, hold your cup like a good girl.'

'No, please . . .'

'Formercysake, hold it still. Imagine, nerves at your age! Me, I can shake like a leaf, I've got reasons. Oh, Lordy, have I got 'em.'

'But . . .'

A dangerous smile tipped the woman's face hideously awry. 'What's the matter? Don't you think I'm good enough to drink with?'

'Please, don't misunderstand,' said Kay, a tremor in her voice. 'It's just that I don't like being forced to do something I don't want to. So look, couldn't I give this to the gentleman?'

'Him? No sirree: he needs what little sense he's got. Come on, honey, down the hatch.'

Kay, seeing it was useless, decided to succumb and avoid a possible scene. She sipped and shuddered. It was terrible gin. It burned her throat till her eyes watered. Quickly, when the woman was not watching, she emptied the cup out into the sound hole of the guitar. It happened, however, that the man saw; and Kay, realizing it, recklessly signalled to him with her eyes a plea not to give her away. But she could not tell from his clear-blank expression how much he understood.

'Where you from, kid?' resumed the woman presently.

For a bewildered moment, Kay was unable to provide an answer. The names of several cities came to her all at once. Finally, from this confusion, she extracted: 'New Orleans. My home is in New Orleans.'

The woman beamed. 'N.O.'s where I wanna go when I kick off. One time, oh, say 1923, I ran me a sweet little fortune-teller parlour there. Let's see, that was on St Peter Street.' Pausing, she stooped and set the empty gin bottle on the floor. It rolled into the aisle and rocked back and forth with a drowsy sound. 'I was raised in Texas – on a big ranch – my papa was rich. Us kids always had the best; even Paris, France, clothes. I'll bet you've got a big swell house, too. Do you have a garden? Do you grow flowers?'

'Just lilacs.'

A conductor entered the coach, preceded by a cold gust of wind that rattled the trash in the aisle and briefly livened the dull air. He lumbered along, stopping now and then to punch a ticket or talk with a passenger. It was after midnight. Someone was expertly playing a harmonica. Someone else was arguing the merits of a certain politician. A child cried out in his sleep.

'Maybe you wouldn't be so snotty if you knew who we was,' said the woman, bobbing her tremendous head. 'We ain't nobodies, not by a long shot.'

Embarrassed, Kay nervously opened a pack of cigarettes and lighted one. She wondered if there might not be a seat in a car up ahead. She could not bear the woman, or, for that matter, the man, another minute. But she had never before been in a remotely comparable situation. 'If you'll excuse me now,' she said, 'I have to be leaving. It's been very pleasant, but I promised to meet a friend on the train. . . .'

With almost invisible swiftness the woman grasped the girl's wrist. 'Didn't your mama ever tell you it was sinful to lie?' she stage-whispered. The lavender hat tumbled off her head but

she made no effort to retrieve it. Her tongue flicked out and
wetted her lips. And, as Kay stood up, she increased the pressure of her grip. 'Sit down, dear ... there ain't any friend ...
Why, we're your only friends and we wouldn't have you leave
us for the world.'

'Honestly, I wouldn't lie.'

'Sit down, dear.'

Kay dropped her cigarette and the man picked it up. He
slouched in the corner and became absorbed in blowing a chain
of lush smoke rings that mounted upward like hollow eyes and
expanded into nothing.

'Why, you wouldn't want to hurt his feelings by leaving us,
now, would you, dear?' crooned the woman softly. 'Sit down
– down – now, that's a good girl. My, what a pretty guitar.
What a pretty, pretty guitar ...' Her voice faded before the
sudden whooshing, static noise of a second train. And for an
instant the lights on the coach went off; in the darkness the
passing train's golden windows winked black-yellow-black-
yellow-black-yellow. The man's cigarette pulsed like the glow
of a firefly, and his smoke rings continued rising tranquilly.
Outside, a bell pealed wildly.

When the lights came on again, Kay was massaging her
wrist where the woman's strong fingers had left a painful
bracelet mark. She was more puzzled than angry. She deter-
mined to ask the conductor if he would find her a different
seat. But when he arrived to take her ticket, the request stutter-
ed on her lips incoherently.

'Yes, miss?'

'Nothing,' she said.

And he was gone.

The trio in the alcove regarded one another in mysterious
silence till the woman said, 'I've got something here I wanna
show you, honey.' She rummaged once more in the oilcloth
satchel. 'You won't be so snotty after you get a gander at
this.'

What she passed to Kay was a handbill, published on such
yellowed, antique paper it looked as if it must be centuries old.
In fragile, overly fancy lettering, it read:

LAZARUS

THE MAN WHO IS BURIED ALIVE
A MIRACLE
SEE FOR YOURSELF

Adults, 25c – Children, 10c

'I always sing a hymn and read a sermon,' said the woman.
'It's awful sad: some folks cry, especially the old ones. And
I've got me a perfectly elegant costume: a black veil and a
black dress, oh, very becoming. *He* wears a gorgeous made-to-
order bridegroom suit and a turban and lotsa talcum on his
face. See, we try to make it as much like a bonafide funeral as
we can. But shoot, nowadays, you're likely to get just a buncha
smart alecks come for laughs – so sometimes I'm real glad he's
afflicted like he is on accounta otherwise his feelings would be
hurt, maybe.'

Kay said, 'You mean you're with a circus or a side-show or
something like that?'

'Nope, us alone,' said the woman as she reclaimed the fallen
hat. 'We've been doing it for years and years – played every
tank town in the South: Singasong, Mississippi – Spunky,
Louisiana – Eureka, Alabama ...' these and other names
rolled off her tongue musically, running together like rain.
'After the hymn, after the sermon, we bury him.'

'In a coffin?'

'Sort of. It's gorgeous, it's got silver stars painted all over
the lid.'

'I should think he would suffocate,' said Kay, amazed. 'How
long does he stay buried?'

'All told it takes maybe an hour – course that's not counting
the lure.'

'The lure?'

'Uh huh. It's what we do the night before the show. See,
we hunt up a store, any ol' store with a big glass window'll do,
and get the owner to let *him* sit inside this window, and, well,
hypnotize himself. Stays there all night stiff as a poker and

133

people come and look: scares the livin' hell out of 'em....'
While she talked she jiggled a finger in her ear, withdrawing it
occasionally to examine her find. 'And one time this ol' bindle-
stiff Mississippi sheriff tried to ...'

The tale that followed was baffling and pointless: Kay did
not bother to listen. Nevertheless, what she had heard already
inspired a reverie, a vague recapitulation of her uncle's funeral;
an event which, to tell the truth, had not much affected her
since she had scarcely known him. And so, while gazing ab-
stractedly at the man, an image of her uncle's face, white next
the pale silk casket pillow, appeared in her mind's eye. Obser-
ving their faces simultaneously, both the man's and uncle's, as
it were, she thought she recognized an odd parallel: there was
about the man's face the same kind of shocking, embalmed,
secret stillness, as though, in a sense, he were truly an exhibit in
a glass cage, complacent to be seen, uninterested in seeing.

'I'm sorry, what did you say?'

'I said: I sure wish they'd lend us the use of a regular ceme-
tery. Like it is now we have to put on the show wherever we
can ... mostly in empty lots that are nine times outa ten smack
up against some smelly fillin' station, which ain't exactly a big
help. But like I say, we got us a swell act, the best. You oughta
come see it if you get a chance.'

'Oh, I should love to,' Kay, said, absently.

'Oh, I should love to,' mimicked the woman. 'Well, who
asked you? Anybody ask you?' She hoisted up her skirt and
enthusiastically blew her nose on the ragged hem of a petticoat.
'Bu-leeve me, it's a hard way to turn a dollar. Know what our
take was last month? Fifty-three bucks! Honey, you try living
on that sometime.' She sniffed and rearranged her skirt with
considerable primness. 'Well, one of these days my sweet boy's
sure enough going to die down there; and even then
somebody'll say it was a gyp.'

At this point the man took from his pocket what seemed to
be a finely shellacked peach seed and balanced it on the palm
of his hand. He looked across at Kay and, certain of her attention, opened his eyelids wide and began to squeeze and caress
the seed in an undefinably obscene manner.

Kay frowned. 'What does he want?'

'He wants you to buy it.'

'But what is it?'

'A charm,' said the woman. 'A love charm.'

Whoever was playing the harmonica stopped. Other sounds, less unique, became at once prominent: someone snoring, the gin bottle seesaw rolling, voices in sleepy argument, the train wheels' distant hum.

'Where could you get love cheaper, honey?'

'It's nice. I mean it's cute. . . .' Kay said, stalling for time. The man rubbed and polished the seed on his trouser leg. His head was lowered at a supplicating, mournful angle, and presently he stuck the seed between his teeth and bit it, as if it were a suspicious piece of silver. 'Charms always bring me bad luck. And besides . . . please, can't you make him stop acting that way?'

'Don't look so scared,' said the woman, more flat-voiced than ever. 'He ain't gonna hurt you.'

'Make him stop, damn it!'

'What can I do?' asked the woman, shrugging her shoulders. 'You're the one that's got money. You're rich. All he wants is a dollar, one dollar.'

Kay tucked her purse under her arm. 'I have just enough to get back to school,' she lied, quickly rising and stepping out into the aisle. She stood there a moment, expecting trouble. But nothing happened.

The woman, with rather deliberate indifference, heaved a sigh and closed her eyes; gradually the man subsided and stuck the charm back in his pocket. Then his hand crawled across the seat to join the woman's in a lax embrace.

Kay shut the door and moved to the front of the observation platform. It was bitterly cold in the open air, and she had left her raincoat in the alcove. She loosened her scarf and draped it over her head.

Although she had never made this trip before, the train was travelling through an area strangely familiar: tall trees, misty, painted pale by malicious moonshine, towered steep on either side without a break or clearing. Above, the sky was a stark, unexplorable blue thronged with stars that faded here and there. She could see streamers of smoke trailing from the train's engine like long clouds of ectoplasm. In one corner of the platform a red kerosene lantern cast a colourful shadow.

She found a cigarette and tried to light it: the wind snuffed match after match till only one was left. She walked to the corner where the lantern burned and cupped her hands to protect the last match: the flame caught, sputtered, died. Angrily she tossed away the cigarette and empty folder; all the tension in her tightened to an exasperating pitch and she slammed the wall with her fist and began to whimper softly, like an irritable child.

The intense cold made her head ache, and she longed to go back inside the warm coach and fall asleep. But she couldn't, at least not yet; and there was no sense in wondering why, for she knew the answer very well. Aloud, partly to keep her teeth from chattering and partly because she needed the reassurance of her own voice, she said: 'We're in Alabama now, I think, and tomorrow we'll be in Atlanta and I'm nineteen and I'll be twenty in August and I'm a sophomore. . . .' She glanced around at the darkness, hoping to see a sign of dawn, and finding the same endless wall of trees, the same frosty moon. 'I hate him, he's horrible and I hate him. . . .' She stopped, ashamed of her foolishness and too tired to evade the truth: she was afraid.

Suddenly she felt an eerie compulsion to kneel down and touch the lantern. Its graceful glass funnel was warm, and the red glow seeped through her hands, making them luminous. The heat thawed her fingers and tingled along her arms.

She was so preoccupied she did not hear the door open. The train wheels roaring clickety-clack-clackety-click hushed the sound of the man's footsteps.

It was a subtle zero sensation that warned her finally; but some seconds passed before she dared look behind.

He was standing there with mute detachment, his head tilted, his arms dangling at his sides. Staring up into his harmless, vapid face, flushed brilliant by the lantern light, Kay knew of what she was afraid: it was a memory, a childish memory of terrors that once, long ago, had hovered above her like haunted limbs on a tree of night. Aunts, cooks, strangers – each eager to spin a tale or teach a rhyme of spooks and death, omens, spirits, demons. And always there had been the unfailing threat of the wizard man: stay close to the house, child, else a wizard man'll snatch you and eat you alive! He lived everywhere, the wizard man, and everywhere was danger. At night, in bed, hear him tapping at the window? Listen!

Holding onto the railing, she inched upward till she was standing erect. The man nodded and waved his hand towards the door. Kay took a deep breath and stepped forward. Together they went inside.

The air in the coach was numb with sleep: a solitary light now illuminated the car, creating a kind of artificial dusk. There was no motion but the train's sluggish sway, and the stealthy rattle of discarded newspapers.

The woman alone was wide awake. You could see she was greatly excited: she fidgeted with her curls and celluloid cherries, and her plump little legs, crossed at the ankles, swung agitatedly back and forth. She paid no attention when Kay sat down. The man settled in the seat with one leg tucked beneath him and his arms folded across his chest.

In an effort to be casual, Kay picked up a magazine. She realized the man was watching her, not removing his gaze an instant: she knew this though she was afraid to confirm it, and she wanted to cry out and waken everyone in the coach. But suppose they did not hear? What if they were not really *asleep*? Tears started in her eyes, magnifying and distorting the print on a page till it became a hazy blur. She shut the magazine with fierce abruptness and looked at the woman.

'I'll buy it,' she said. 'The charm, I mean. I'll buy it, if that's all – just all you want.'

The woman made no response. She smiled apathetically as she turned towards the man.

As Kay watched, the man's face seemed to change form and recede before her like a moon-shaped rock sliding downward under a surface of water. A warm laziness relaxed her. She was dimly conscious of it when the woman took away her purse, and when she gently pulled the raincoat like a shroud above her head.

More about Penguins and Pelicans

Penguinews, which appears every month, contains details of all the new books issued by Penguins as they are published. From time to time it is supplemented by *Penguins in Print*, which is our complete list of almost 5,000 titles.

A specimen copy of *Penguinews* will be sent to you free on request. Please write to Dept EP, Penguin Books Ltd, Harmondsworth, Middlesex, for your copy.

In the U.S.A.: For a complete list of books available from Penguins in the United States write to Dept CS, Penguin Books, 625 Madison Avenue, New York, New York 10022.

In Canada: For a complete list of books available from Penguins in Canada write to Penguin Books Canada Ltd, 2801 John Street, Markham, Ontario L3R 1B4.

The Grass Harp

Truman Capote

By the author of *In Cold Blood* – the most discussed book on both sides of the Atlantic for twenty years.

Two old women and a boy up a tree; the sheriff, the judge, and the massed might of the would-be dignitaries of an American small town advancing, shotguns under arm, through the wood ...

Sensation! The judge defects to the other side. Why, says he, shouldn't these gentle, honest people go and live in a tree house if they want to?

Clicking of safety catches ...

This one must be the funniest, happiest, and most captivating of Truman Capote's novels.

Breakfast at Tiffany's

Truman Capote

Miss Holiday Golightly

Travelling

That was how the card on her door used to read. For Holly, Truman Capote's unforgettable good-time girl, was always on the move. It is one of her past admirers who recalls without sentimentality his acquaintance with this gay, pragmatical, wary, and utterly tragic human meteorite with her 'breakfast-cereal' air of health.

'Contains in full that delicate exactness of perception that has made Mr Capote so famous so young' – John Metcalf in the *Sunday Times*

'Places him at once among the leading American writers of the day' – *The Times Literary Supplement*